SHAMELESSLY LOYAL

82ND STREET VANDALS CROSSOVER NOVELLA

BAY RIDGE ROYALS
BOOK ONE

HEATHER LONG

Shamelessly Loyal/Heather Long – 1st ed.

ISBN: 978-1-956264-71-5

For Mayhem.
She knows why.

SERIES SO FAR

Shamelessly Loyal (Novella)
Battle Lines

Savage Vandal
Vicious Rebel
Ruthless Traitor
Dirty Devil
Shamelessly Loyal (Novella)
Brutal Fighter

FOREWORD

Dear Reader,

Welcome to Shamelessly Loyal. You may have noticed that this is listed as book 1 for Bay Ridge Royals, but it's also labeled as a crossover novella between Bay Ridge Royals *and* 82nd Street Vandals (more on them in a sec). While true, the crossover aspects involves events kicked off in Vandals that bring these characters together.

This book focuses on two specific PoV characters: Lainey and Milo. Future books in the series will include multiple PoVs for all main characters. While this particular novella focuses on the m/f relationship that develops between two characters, future books in this series will add others into the mix. (IYKYK).

This novella is set during *Dirty Devil* and *Brutal Fighter*, books 4 and 5 of the 82nd Street Vandals. You do *not* need to have read this series to enjoy this novella. We are following two fan-favorite characters to see what they were doing while the Vandals were focused on Emersyn.

If you do decide to check out 82nd Street Vandals, be sure to start with *Savage Vandal*. This novella may contain some spoilers for the first three books of that series, so just a heads up.

This novella originally appeared in Billionaires and Babes, an anthology for the Ballgowns and Books Events used to raise money for charity. There are some slight differences and a couple of additional scenes added to the novella at the beginning and end. The majority of this remains as presented in the anthology.

For a little housekeeping. Bay Ridge Royals is a why choose with multiple new adults exploring and coming to terms with their evolving sexuality, identities, and relationships.

TWs: Mentions of SA. Mentions of CSA. Kidnapping. Threats of violence. Discussion of trafficking. Be kind to yourself, this is the first start of a new dark romance series that also serves as a bridge to another dark romance series.

Thanks for checking out Milo and Lainey, I can't wait for you to get to know them.

Happy reading.

xoxo

Heather

THE VANDALS

82nd Street Boys
   Jasper "Hawk" Horan
   Kellan "Kestrel" Traschel
   Rome "Hummingbird" Cleary
   Vaughn "Falcon" Westbrook
   Liam "Mockingbird" O'Connell
   Freddie "Unknown" Cleary
   Milo "Raptor" Hardigan
   Mickey "Doc" James aka Vandal
   Emersyn "Dove, Sparrow, Starling, Swan, Little Bit, Boo-Boo, Hellspawn, Ivy" Sharpe

Other Characters
   Elaine "Lainey" Benedict
   Adam Reed
   Ezra Graham
   Ms. Stephanie

PROLOGUE

LAINEY

A FEW YEARS EARLIER...

I checked my watch as the car pulled into the transit station. It was my first time going to this one, but I had a map and I'd done my research. I also already had my tickets and the pass required by the company for an unaccompanied minor. It was amazing how easy that was to book. My grandfather's assistant was more than happy to acquire permission for me and arrange transportation. Chances were unless Grandfather asked her directly, she wouldn't mention it because she was used to handling things for me because Mother never did.

The experience would be educational, after all. Fifteen minutes later, I waited patiently with my suitcase to be shown to my compartment on the sleeper car. It would take us about eighteen to twenty hours to get in, and booking the overnight gave me more time. The school would take a couple of days to notice my absence.

They would wait at least twenty-four to thirty-six hours after that before they notified Mother. Depending on her mood, it could be a week before she took any action. I would be back *long* before then. I was more than capable of handling the trip.

As it was, more than one adult had peered at me curiously. If they stared for too long, I would look across the area to find someone farther away and flash a smile before I started toward them. Inevitably, it worked, distracted adults seemed to think that as long as I *appeared* to be with another adult, it was fine and they could ignore me.

It didn't matter. I would be locked into my sleeper compartment soon. I'd brought books, a snack, and my phone. All I wanted to do was arrive in time to celebrate my best friend's birthday. I couldn't *wait* to surprise her. She had a very brief hiatus and this was an impulsive call on my part.

Either way, I was so excited. I barely slept all night but I finished two books and I finally managed a nap after the sun came up and woke when the porter knocked just a half hour before the station. My car and driver were waiting for me.

I loved tourist cities. It made impulsive planning that much easier. As soon as I got to the hotel, I informed the desk I was there to check into my room but my roommate was probably already there and I had no idea if the room was in my name or hers.

The desk clerk gave me a steady look until I identified my best friend by her "incognito" name. Emersyn Sharpe would earn too much attention and not the least of which because she was a performer. No, better to keep the details private. Yes, my best friend had checked in *and* had the extra key.

I'd caught a reflection of the room number on the desk clerk's glasses and made a show of checking my phone when the clerk said she needed to call up because my name *wasn't* on the room. No, that would definitely *not* do. I wanted to surprise Em.

Surprising her was the whole point of this trip.

"Oh, she just texted me." I added her room number with a grin. "Thank you! Sorry to have bothered you."

"Not at all," she assured me, relief filling her eyes. "You want to use those elevators over there..."

I gave her a little wave as I took the elevator up and then followed the signs to Em's room. All of my decorum fled when I knocked on her door.

"What the—" The words sounded from the other side of the door and my smile grew as the locks tumbled free and then Em was there. "Lainey!"

Real joy ripped through me at her shock and happiness. Nothing artificial ever existed between me and Em. Nothing. She was—she was my best friend for a reason. Her hug enveloped me and I held her as tightly as I could.

"What are you doing here?" The demand made me laugh as Em dragged me inside. This—her simple happiness at seeing me—was why I'd come all this way. But it wasn't the *only* reason. I wanted to *see* her. In my world, everyone wanted something. Every relationship was transactional and required an understanding of what they wanted versus what I was willing to give up.

Em?

It was just different. Different, and precious and absolutely mine. I wouldn't share her with anyone. If that meant I was in deep shit when I got back, fine.

Worth it.

It was her birthday and I only had a short window of time that let me be here *with* her. So we were going to take every advantage. Here, I wasn't Elaine Benedict and she wasn't Emersyn Sharpe. We could be whoever we wanted to be and I wanted to be with my best friend and having fun.

I wanted to be—*us*.

We got changed and went downstairs. I had my travel card, so I sprang for tickets to the park including the party that they were having that night. "No rules," I reminded Em when she'd given me that wide-eyed look. The elegance of the cages around us had never been lost on me.

Whether we entered them voluntarily or not, we always returned to them. We would again, unfortunately, but later.

Much later.

The hours flew by as we shopped, got on rides—sometimes two and three times in a row, ate terrible for us food, and watched shows. We even got play costumes so we could trick or treat. Villains, not princesses. The parades though, they were the best. After the fireworks, we finally headed back to the hotel.

I was tired. Em was tired. It had been an amazing day. No sooner did we leave the bus and head toward the hotel entrance than a pair of my worst nightmares appeared.

Really? *Now*? They couldn't have waited another day?

"Oh, you've got to be *kidding* me." I did not want them here.

Adam Reed, the son of the man my mother acted as mistress for. I adored Adam's mother, she was a kind woman. The absolute best. His father was awful and Adam couldn't decide which parent to take after. Worse, he randomly decided he was the boss of me one day and seemed to make it his mission in life to control everything I did.

No, thank you.

Next to him? Ezra Graham. Clearly, because where else would Ezra be. He didn't have a single thought of his own that Adam didn't allow him. Except—every once in a while when Adam was absent, Ezra seemed to rediscover he had a soul.

Today was not going to be that day.

"Ignore them," I told Em when she suddenly put herself between me and them. The utterly selfless act didn't take into account how dangerous those two were. I'd seen them do some truly awful things, but I understood discretion. Maybe a lot more than they knew.

"Who is he?" Em asked and Adam flicked her a dismissive look before he focused on me. Yes, he hated the Sharpes. I was aware. He still didn't get to tell me who my friends were.

"Do you have any idea how long it took me to find you?" Adam practically growled.

"Not long enough," I informed him. How had they even known I left the school? They should have only just *now* noticed my absence. This was not acceptable. I'd been careful in my planning. "And this is my mother's lover's son, or as I like to refer to him the human version of period cramps."

Ezra burst out laughing, despite Adam's glower. So happy I could entertain. Now, to get Em back inside safe and sound.

"If you wanted to come see your friend," Adam said finally, sparing her a brief look before he focused on me again. "You should have just said something."

"Adam Reed, I don't have to tell you anything. In case

you missed the memo, let me be clear, you're like a cloud. A big, dark, ugly storm cloud and when you go away, it's a beautiful day. So, buh bye." I ignored the reproach in his eyes that quickly tumbled right back to fury.

Pissing him off had become my personal hobby even when I didn't *want* to make him angry. He was always angry with me. I guided Em past him and did my best to ignore the snickers and snorts from Ezra. I had to wonder if he had been drinking or doing something else recreationally.

Nothing in this conversation was funny.

"We came all this way and we're not leaving until your ass is in the car with us and on the way back to school," Adam informed me.

"Sorry, my ass doesn't detach—unlike your personality. Maybe you should put a bag over it or something," I tossed the last comment over my shoulder as we went inside. All the way to the elevator, they shadowed us.

Apparently my lack of cooperation stymied them.

"Six in the morning," Adam ordered. "Meet us down here and don't try to sneak off somewhere."

"Six?" I snorted. "Too bad your brains don't match your looks. I'll be down by ten." I kept my composure as the doors closed and then added, "Maybe." All the way until the doors themselves shut, I'd expected Adam to just pick me up and march off.

He'd done that before. I was pretty capable, but he was a lot bigger than me. I didn't want him to scare Em.

"That's Adam?" Surprise flickered in Em's voice. She knew who Adam and Ezra were. I'd told her about them.

"That's Adam," I confirmed.

I used to have the biggest crush on them both. Adam had been my hero in some ways. Then one day, he'd turned into a demon and hated having anything to do with me. Yet, here he was, following me around.

Again.

"He must care if he came all this way." The hope in Em's voice made me sad.

"Adam lives to make my life hell. So, if he wants to wait until morning. He can wait. It's your birthday and we're here to celebrate." I would fight them every step of the way if they tried to make me leave. "You shower first," I told her. "I'll get room service."

I waited for her to get in the shower. I made the call for room service. They said that they already had the order, including the birthday cake.

Dammit, Adam.

I left her a quick note for Em having to go down for the room service. It was a little lie. But I wanted to check in with Adam and Ezra without Em to hear any of their cutting or abrasive comments.

Downstairs, they weren't in the bar, but I spotted Ezra stalking out the doors in a fury. Fine, I followed him. The last thing I expected was to find them fighting with—the guy looked familiar. I didn't know him, but I could have sworn I did...

Then Adam and Ezra were trying to body slam him. All the blows they rained down and they looked more damaged than he did. The head butt he delivered to Ezra sent Ezra sprawling and then the pretty boy fell over the curb. Adam was going to kill him. He barely managed to dodge Adam's next flurry of blows and I jumped in between them.

"What are you doing?" I shrieked.

"Get your ass back in the hotel," Adam growled at me. Pretty Boy retreated behind me even as Adam kept cutting his gaze from me to behind me then back. They were all bruised and bleeding.

"No," I said, folding my arms. What the hell was wrong with them? They follow me here and now they were beating some stranger up?

"Excuse me?" Adam took one step toward me then his attention snapped up to the guy who was behind me. This wasn't the safest place for me to stand but it did keep Adam and Ezra from continuing to hurt this guy.

"You heard me," I yelled at him. "Have you lost your mind? Fighting out here? Why are you guys beating this guy up? Do you want to get arrested? Cause if you want that, I'll call the cops. Right. Now."

Ezra snorted a laugh, the blood running down his face far from attractive. "Fuck me, Lainey don't be such a little bitch."

Adam swung around, only this time, he slammed his fist into Ezra and knock him on his ass. I almost wished I could take the time to enjoy that. Almost. Then Adam was glaring at me again.

"Fine. Get back in the hotel."

"Not without you two. I apparently can't trust you and I came down to thank you for Emersyn's cake. I was going to actually ask if you wanted to join us but you're not going up there all bloody and gross." Not all of that was true.

But... it was true enough.

A half-laugh sounded behind me and I pivoted to face the idiot who was *still* standing there. I had them distracted. Did he lack even basic survival skills?

"I don't know who you are or where you came from. But now is the time you go—*while* I have them distracted." He shifted his stance and the light illuminated just how battered and reddened half of his beautiful face had become. "Oh my god, what did you do to his pretty face?"

Should I get him something for it? I barely took a step forward when Adam snarled all over again. "Lainey. On the count of three, if you aren't moving in the direction of that hotel, I'm throwing your ass in our car and going home. One..."

He would do it too. I felt bad for Pretty Boy but I wasn't losing the rest of Em's birthday.

"Jerk." I glared at Adam then glanced at their target. "Sorry, I never get to see my best friend."

"Two." Was he for real? Counting like I was a toddler or something.

"You really are period cramps," I snapped at him and then stomped back inside. I glanced back *once* to make sure that they left Pretty Boy alone. Ezra was still on his ass and out on the concrete.

Huh.

Adam must have really belted him. Good,

I stole a look toward Pretty Boy again. I hoped he was okay. Adam and Ezra were very dangerous people. No matter how they tried to play it. Grandfather reminded me, regularly, appreciate people for exactly who they were. Them being a threat? It would be a mistake to believe anything else.

With a sigh, I headed for the elevator and escaped back upstairs. I wanted to make the most of every moment we had left.

The next day would be here soon enough.

CHAPTER
ONE

LAINEY

The pair—Rome and Freddie—were equal parts fascinating and frustrating. Both blond, one far more stoic and literal than the other, and utterly different in their mannerisms and how they communicated. Rome said very little but meant every single word. Freddie never shut up and meant maybe one in ten.

They both wanted to help Emersyn. It was all I needed to know. Turning my head to the window, I studied the city we approached. Joining them in their vehicle had been an impulsive decision—one I didn't usually allow myself. But I was worried about Em. She'd disappeared for months. The whole world hunted for her. Out of the blue, she messaged me for help.

Then, almost as abruptly, seemed to change her mind and stay where she was. Now? Now they said she'd gone home.

To her family.

If that were true, the Sharpes would close ranks, and I'd

never get to her. But there was something about these men. Something about the risk they'd taken. I had a gun in my bag, but neither had lied to me. Neither had tried to dismiss my concern.

That worried me even more.

Wherever we were going was where I needed to be.

I wanted answers, and I wanted my best friend back.

I was damn well going to get both.

The drive took longer than I liked, although it passed more swiftly than it seemed.

Once in the city itself, our destination proved to be nearer the ports than the suburbs. Right in the heart of a poorer area littered with condemned buildings, struggling businesses, and the vagaries of slow but steady urban redevelopment. The kind that would gentrify the area.

Most saw that as a boon, but the current populace would be pushed out. The deeper we went, the more obvious it became. Some of these storefronts were decades old. Then we were suddenly pulling up to a warehouse.

They lived in a warehouse?

Surprise fluttered through me even as my curiosity pricked me. Why a warehouse? What were the benefits? The drawbacks? Tactically, was this even safe? The roll-up door confirmed my supposition and then my stoic driver pulled in. Freddie shot a glance over his shoulder.

"Give me five minutes to smooth the way."

He bounced out of the car before the roll door behind us even closed. I didn't reach for the door handle. Rome, the driver, had engaged the child-proof locks—like that wasn't a little humiliating—so I had to wait for him to open the door for me. He didn't wait five minutes, though.

"Cooperate," he said, though it sounded more like a suggestion than an order.

"Or?" I challenged him as I stepped out of the car.

"Or this will take longer than it needs, and Starling doesn't have time for that, correct?"

Rebellion died a swift and silent death. "Correct."

With a nod, he closed the door and I glanced around the warehouse. "You live here?" Assuming control offered me a measure of comfort. I was here by *my* choice. Not theirs. I was here as an *ally*, not to just hand off responsibility. The men who clustered together, and suddenly seemed very focused on me, needed to understand this sooner rather than later.

"Rome?" one of the men asked.

"She's a friend of Starling's." Well, that was succinct. The name Starling seemed almost ethereal and rather precious for Emersyn. However, she was not that fragile.

"Why the *fuck* is she here?" That voice.

I knew that voice. I searched the faces of the men glowering at me.

"Because I want to be," I snapped in response, closing the distance between us. Frankly, I needed the walk and the stretch. But I wanted to find him. What the hell was Pretty Boy doing *here*? "These idiots didn't tell me we were a two-day drive from where we needed to be. I could have gotten us here a lot faster, not to mention we'll need to move faster if this is going to work at all."

I studied each of them in turn, but it wasn't until I found his face that the recognition not only struck me but truly registered.

What she'd said about the group. What she'd described. The words I'd managed to squeeze out of my escort. Pretty Boy was here. More... "*You're* her brother?"'

No one said a word, yet the man smoking a cigarette cut

13

his gaze past me and the "brother" I stared at. "Freddie, what the fuck did you two do?"

"We're working on getting Boo-Boo back. She has information. She's kind of bitchy if you interrupt her, so just let her talk."

"Freddie," Pretty Boy snapped. "We don't kidnap women."

"No, we just kidnap Boo-Boo."

That was almost entertaining.

"We didn't kidnap her." The stoic one only parted with a few words at a time.

"They didn't *kidnap* me." We really didn't have time for this, or my shock. How and why Pretty Boy was here would have to wait for later. If he was her brother, his presence in Florida years earlier made sense. But still...

A door slammed, and a carbon copy of the stoic one strode across the intervening distance at a ground-eating pace that promised death and destruction were riding in with him. I'd seen that kind of expression before.

While Pretty Boy looked like he planned to intervene, the newcomer wasn't remotely interested. Nevertheless, the closer he came, the more familiar he looked. He was Rome's twin, so that made sense. The familiarity was annoying, as were the interruptions. There were too many people here to wrangle.

What had Em been thinking?

"What the hell did you do, Rome? Why would you bring Elaine Benedict *here* of all places?" the newcomer demanded.

How nice, he knew exactly who I was. Fine, I could work with that. "Great, is there anyone else coming who is going to be shocked and awed by my presence that we'll need to stop to explain it all?" I demanded. "If so, would it be possible to use the restroom now? I'd rather discuss *Emersyn's* problems instead of this, but we don't have all day."

"She can help," Rome said after I finished. "Come on, I'll show you to the bathroom."

"Wait," his snarling brother said before we even went two steps. "Having *her* here is dangerous."

"Why?" the smoker demanded.

"Fuck this," one of the men stated. "Rome - take her to the bathroom. Everyone else, shut up and let Freddie explain. All of you, be quick. We'll do this inside— Vaughn, call Doc and get him over here. Then we won't have to have them explain everything twice."

Rome dipped his head to the door, and I didn't waste time on listening to their debate. I needed to do more than just empty my bladder. He guided me upstairs, then through a bedroom to another room. "This is Starling's," he said. "The bathroom is clean."

Honestly, I'd take it. "Thank you."

Once in the bathroom with the door closed, I leaned back against it. Steadying my breathing and my pulse took some significant focus. Starling's room—Em's. This had been her room. Her bathroom.

A scant investigation didn't turn up anything familiar. I made use of the toilet, then washed up. I needed a real shower and change, but that would have to wait. As it was, I made do with freshening up and then checked my cosmetics. Despite the nearly two days in the back of the car, I was only slightly rumpled.

Ten minutes later, I had my heart rate steady and my breathing even. The touch-up smoothed out my expression, and when I opened the door to the bathroom. I was ready to deal with these strangers. They cared about Emersyn.

That was a huge mark in their favor. Danger radiated from every single one. Danger and suspicion.

I didn't care about that, not as long as it meant they'd do anything to get Emersyn back. Downstairs, the silence crackled with all the things they weren't saying. Freddie had fixed sandwiches, a lot of sandwiches. He offered them to me like they were hors d'oeuvre and I debated declining.

However, my stomach cramped in protest, so I selected one of the ham and cheese sandwiches with a nod. The sincerity in his grin was kind of painful. Everything about him screamed youth and pain, yet he was genuinely trying. More than once, I caught the men staring at me, studying me, weighing me. I kept my expression under control.

Grandfather often said that when you can control your body language, you can control a room. Always leave them wanting more and *needing* to understand. Here, that seemed prescient advice.

I had taken a seat while we waited, not because I wanted to surrender any control in letting them tower over me but because I needed them to calm down. As it was, the twin's brother vibrated with barely leashed rage and kept glaring at the door more than me. So, whoever we were waiting on—the elusive Doc—was definitely the subject of his ire. When the door opened, admitting the older man with the hollow eyes and the tight expression, the angry twin snapped his glare to me.

"Talk."

"Charming, I'd know you two were brothers without the looks." Personally, I preferred stoicism and minimal use of words to testosterone-fueled anger. Uneasy humor rippled through the others, but to be fair, we didn't have time to linger on this. I looked at Freddie. So far, he'd been the most bluntly honest with me. "Everyone here is trustworthy?"

"Yes," he answered without equivocation.

"Good, because I'm going to need all of you to help." Now, however, I rose from my seat and moved to stand in front of the dark television. It allowed me to control where they directed their attention and gave me a clear line of sight to all of them. "Emersyn's in trouble."

"And you know this—" Dammit, the raw growl of anger in his voice should not be remotely compelling.

Still, I cut her brother off with a slice of my hand. "Pretty Boy, this will go much faster if you let me talk and save the questions until after the presentation."

Shock punched the silence and his jaw snapped closed with an audible click and the grind of teeth. It really should make him less attractive. The darkness clinging to my pretty boy disturbed me a hell of a lot more than I wanted to admit—to anyone.

"So, a little more this," I continued, holding my thumb and fingers together like a closed mouth. "Instead of this." I mimed yapping with my hand. His eyes went flat and dark. His eyes. This close, there was no mistaking Emersyn's eyes glaring out at me. Only the storm and fury in them had never been directed at me. "Good. Emersyn contacted me a few days ago because of a reward that was put out by my family and friends of ours. I knew she was okay, but my grandfather offered the reward at my request. We were hoping someone would try to collect from us before the Sharpes, and that would let me know if anyone had found her before they could sell her out."

I needed to tell them everything. Even revealing the gaps in what I knew. Holding back now wouldn't help her. That wasn't an option.

Folding my arms, I pressed on. "I promised her I would help in any way. I would also warn her if we heard anything. That was our last conversation. Then I heard she'd been *found* and was coming home."

Revulsion slid through me. The few scant images I'd seen of her at the airport had terrified me. Her uncle was— revolting. Going home was *not* what she wanted. Ever.

"That was the last thing she wanted."

"Told you," Freddie said, though his tone was far from smug.

"You sound certain," Pretty Boy said, though there was less challenge in his tone now.

"That's because I am, I've known Emersyn since we were five. Granted—we haven't always been in the same places, and we had a hard time keeping in touch sometimes. Nonetheless, we never gave up on each other, and I'm *not* giving up on her now. As much as I hated not knowing exactly where she was, I was happy knowing she was *safe.*"

And I had wanted to press her a dozen times, but she'd seemed so sure...

"She never told me why you took her, and I don't care right now. I'm just glad you did. Her going back was never the plan."

"The fake IDs," Liam said abruptly. "You got them for her."

"Yes, a new identity, cash, anything she needed to not be Emersyn Sharpe anymore and disappear." I'd gone straight to Fletcher. Adam's cousin was much more laid back than he was, yet he was also clever as Hell and had access to everything I needed. He hadn't even asked me a lot of questions, when I would have paid the full price he insisted on the friends and family discount.

It was for Emersyn, so honestly, I'd have paid it in blood.

"Where is she now?" one of them asked. "Where is she that you're so damn worried about?"

The ice in my veins chilled even further. "If he's done what I think he has, and if the rumors are true, he's sent her back to Pinetree."

"What the hell is Pinetree?" the newcomer demanded.

"It's a psychiatric facility," Liam answered, a muscle ticking in his jaw. "A very exclusive one."

"You've heard of it?" That was useful, because I wasn't sure how to explain the nightmare fuel that place provided to the children and black sheeps of the wealthy circles I traveled in. "All I know is that if she's there, we need to get her out. I have the money and the connections, but I have no way to get in, and I don't think I could anyway—the last two times he sent her to that place—she was different when she came out."

"Different, how?" Pretty Boy invaded my space. Worry, not an ounce of threat stamped on his face. It wrenched at my heart. "There was never anything about her being in a facility."

"Of course not, it wouldn't reflect well on the family. But I knew. Some of us knew, because we saw what happened after. The only reason they sent her there was to control her—to take away who she was, and I couldn't stop it before. I *can* do something now."

"That's where we come in," the big guy said. Like the doctor, he'd said almost nothing.

"Exactly. I just—I just don't know how to make it happen, and I need help to get her out." If I thought for a second Adam would back my play, I'd have gone to him.

Our parents' affair and subsequent marriage aside, we had Andrea in common.

Sometimes I thought she might be all we had; only he wasn't a monster. His concern for Emersyn when we were kids had never been feigned. Nor his concern *about* my friendship with her. I'd have begged if I had to, but he'd all but disappeared over the recent weeks. The one person who might know where he was, wasn't speaking to me. It didn't help either that my last conversation with Ezra had been a drunken rant that still stung.

"Tell them," Rome said, cutting across the sea of debate and argument. He wasn't looking at me or talking to me, for that matter. He was looking at his brother. "It's time, tell them."

I just needed them to help me help her. Their reaching out when they did? It was a lifeline I'd grasped and then dove into the dark water after. Maybe I'd drown, but not before I got her help.

I could do this much.

TWO

MILO

"Y ou wanna tell me why she's locked in your room?" Kellan asked, and I spared him a look. "Or not," he continued. "Keeping *her* here, not your best idea."

Was he for fucking real right now? Lainey Benedict didn't belong in our world, at all. Of course, I would have said Ivy didn't belong here, either. This was *not* what I wanted for Ivy, and that was before I began to vanish into a morally gray area, all in the name of protecting my brothers and building a life worthy of my sister.

The gray I traded for the bankrupt. "Go away, Kel. Fix the shit you can fix and back up the boys so they can find my sister."

He frowned.

"What?"

"Why aren't you going with them?"

Anger lit a match and tore through me like a kerosene-fueled fire. Only I said nothing because *why wasn't I going?* It was a damn good question. I wasn't on parole, so I could leave the state. Ivy needed me...

However, only one answer managed to evade the flames, and it was a brutal truth. "If I go, I'm going to kill every single person standing between me and her. If that is what she needs, then fuck it. We'll burn it all down. But right now—Liam is thinking."

The words, *I can't* scarred my tongue. Rome and Freddie were going with him. They might be wild cards at times, but Rome would have his brother's back and Freddie's in turn. And of all of us, Freddie seemed the least threatening. Only, appearances were truly deceptive.

"Do what you need to do," I told Kellan. "I'll keep an eye on our guest." My sister's best friend. A woman who'd risked an awful lot to bring us the information she had. Maybe making peace with her should be on the agenda. It would have to wait.

Once I got past the need to blister her ass for putting herself in danger. She didn't fucking know us, yet she just got in a car with Rome and Freddie?

"Raptor," Kellan yanked my attention back to him. "You don't have to be the one to look after her. Vaughn or I..."

I narrowed my eyes. The sudden possessiveness bursting inside of me had nothing to do with Ivy and everything to do with the fragile beauty locked in my room. The girl who radiated power, wealth, confidence, and intelligence. The fierce little being who'd bonded with my sister and built a lasting friendship when they were kids. Except, she wasn't a child. Not even close. She was a lady. The kind of lady who would have nothing to do with the rougher side of life, but she marched in here like she was a woman on a mission.

"You find Ivy," I told him. "You straighten out all this

22

shit you said you wanted to take on because we aren't doing it my way anymore." Those words stung, although I deserved them. Walking back into my life had proven more impossible than going into prison in the first place.

"If we're doing it my way," Kellan told me dryly. "Then we send her home."

Fucker was testing me. So I just gave him a tight smile. "Noted."

His chuckle followed me as I headed for the stairs. If not for the lack of humor in his voice, I might have punched him. Brothers tested each other. They pushed each other. They guarded each other's backs. Right now, I needed his attention on Ivy.

I needed *her* back. Even if it didn't mean coming here. Halfway to my room and alone for the first time in hours, my steps faltered. Head down, I clenched my fists. Breathing exercises were bullshit, but the agony of finding Ivy immersed in our world vied a pitched battle with the ache of her *leaving* us to go back to her world—only to find out that world wasn't what it should be.

Snapping my head up, I stared at the door at the end of the hall. The guys hadn't changed a fucking thing in there during my absence. Hell, my old law books and half-finished papers were still on the shelves. Cases I'd been reading for class. A jacket that I'd thrown over the back of a chair before I left.

A fine layer of dust had coated everything. Not only had they locked the room up and left it untouched, but they'd also truly stayed out of it. It was like they'd sealed up the door the day I went to prison. It was a thoughtful gesture that cut deep past the fascia and into the muscle.

It had taken me days to work up the will to clean it. That was after everything blew up in my face with Ivy and

Jasper. Scrubbing a hand over my face, I packed all the emotional garbage away. It didn't do anyone any good. Dust wouldn't kill anyone, and I'd gotten it all.

Fuck, my law books.

Shaking off the poisonous tendrils of melancholy, I resumed my course for the room. One thing prison had drummed into my skull hard—we didn't have time for our feelings or to wallow in self-pity. A moment here or there? Fine. Much more, and you were vulnerable to attack.

I stuffed my hand in my pocket for my keys. I'd never locked my brothers out. Half the time, I forgot there was a lock on the door, only this particular lock was on the outside. The inner lock was pretty fucking feeble. I could kick it in if I really needed to.

Unlocking the deadbolt, I gave the door two firm knocks before I opened it. When I'd left her earlier, she'd given me a look that was pure impatience, particularly when I'd told her to stay put.

Even though I'd braced for it, the angry girl wasn't waiting for me. In fact, the room seemed almost empty. The lights were on and the closet door was wide open, but the bathroom door opened a moment later, letting out steam and a towel-wrapped beauty.

Fuck.

My.

Life.

She was working a towel against her dark, damp hair and had legs for miles. The towel barely hit the tops of her thighs. They were beautiful legs, toned, tanned like she spent time outside, and capped by a pair of delicate feet with pale pink toenails. The contrast in the softer color to her bolder choices held me riveted.

A whistle cut through the air, and I yanked my attention up from her legs to find her watching me with thinly-veiled amusement. "Did you bring my bag with you, Pretty Boy?"

Pretty Boy. I shook my head. "No, I'll get it for you. Though I'd rather put you and the bag back in a car and take you home."

"Sucks to be you, then," she said as she lowered her arm, the towel she'd been using on her hair fisted in one hand. "I'm not leaving unless it's to go to Pinetree and get my best friend."

"That's the last place you need to be."

"You say that like you know me, Pretty Boy. We've met all of once... granted, you left an impression." The whole time she spoke, she crossed the room toward me. The way she moved was pure sensuality, and you'd have thought she was dressed in a power suit rather than a towel.

That had me raising my brows.

"Don't be so impressed. I rarely forget a face, especially not one as pretty as yours." Light fingers drifted down my cheek as she gave me a light pat. "Even if you have changed."

That stilled me, and I caught her hand before she could pull it away. The skin was so damn soft under the roughness of my own. "Don't try to seduce me," I informed her. "It won't work, and the only place I'll be taking you is home. If you choose to remain, then this—" I nodded to the room around us. "This is where you're staying. Where I can be sure you're safe."

She canted her head, tilting it back to meet my gaze. I practically towered over her, not that she seemed remotely moved by the distinct difference in our heights. If anything, she seemed more challenged. Dammit. She was too wealthy and too privileged to understand the real danger.

No sooner did that thought take purchase than I had to admit, she understood enough to seek help for Ivy. Even if it was an untenable risk for her to come to strangers and be at our mercy.

Releasing her abruptly, I took a step back. "I'll get your bag. If you want a shirt or something else until I'm back, help yourself to anything in the closet."

"I can wait. There's something a little too intimate about me wearing your clothes, Pretty Boy." The teasing note in her voice was back, the sensuality threading every syllable wrapped around my cock like a fist and squeezed. "You're going to have to earn that privilege."

A bolt of purely inappropriate lust went through me as I met her gaze. The corners of her mouth tilted, pleasure? Or amusement?

Maybe both.

"Go on," she said, pivoting on her bare foot and sauntering —it was absolutely a saunter. The delectable sway of those hips begged me to put my hands on them and bend her over...

What the fuck?

I cut off that train of thought brutally.

"Problems, Pretty Boy?"

"Stop acting like a whore," I told her, ignoring the cruelty in those words. "Don't pretend to be something you're not."

All at once, she swept the towel away, then put a hand on her hip. "You have a problem with my body? That sounds like a *you* thing and not a me thing. I'm fine with who I am. Now, be a good little boy and go get me my bag."

Without another glance in my direction, she disappeared into the bathroom, taking the acres of smooth, hairless, tanned skin and soft, sweet curves with her.

There wasn't even a hint of a bikini line and my cock was so fucking hard, all I could think about was shutting that beautiful mouth of hers around it and choking her into silence. If she was swallowing my dick, she wasn't going to be giving me lip.

That conjured an image of her on her knees with tears in her eyes and my cum splattered all over her as she begged me for more. The need to walk into that bathroom, drag her back out, and put her on her knees was a visceral burn in my blood. A warning.

For me.

I slammed the door on my way out and turned the lock. Then I strode down the hall, passing Vaughn without a word as he raised his brows. The bag in question was sitting in the living room. One of the guys had to have brought it in. I seized it by the straps, then put it back down.

If I went up there again, I was going to make a decision she would regret—a decision I would loathe. I was not a rapist. No matter what it said on my fucking sentencing papers. Just because her body turned me on was not her fault.

It was mine.

Women were to be protected, admired, cherished, and never fucking abused.

In the kitchen, I tugged open the fridge and pulled out a bottle of beer. No matter what fucking time it was, I knocked the lid off and then drained it all before I grabbed a second.

There had to be some work to do out in the warehouse. I would be close enough to keep an eye on who came and went. No one was getting in my room without the key and they'd have to pry it out of my cold dead fingers before I'd let them get near that girl.

That girl.

Lainey Benedict.

Even her name was a sensual curse in my mind and I could practically feel the dare in her eyes. Fuck I wanted those eyes on me as my cock pulsed between her lips. I took another long slug of cold beer as I stomped out into the warehouse. Rats scattered at my arrival. Little shits had been hanging out, sitting around and a couple even smoked.

The truck was only half unloaded.

Good. I could take this frustration out on them.

"What the fuck do you think we pay you to do?" I demanded, and the guy closest to me paled.

I shouldn't have enjoyed it.

But I did.

A FEW YEARS EARLIER...

I didn't say a word when I checked out where they were going to be. The next show was clear across the country. Only I could make the drive in a couple of days. I'd get there the same day they did. Gas money and a few hundred dollars socked away for a rainy day. Her birthday was coming up. Well, the birthday she celebrated anyway. And I wanted to see her. I was also being selfish as fuck.

For the first time in a long time, I didn't care. I just— needed the break. A break from everything. I needed to see her and have a breather. Leaving a note for the guys, I told them I'd be back in a few days. It was better to slip away unseen, or someone would take it upon themselves to follow me. Or just climb in the car.

Once on the highway, I exhaled a long breath. The agitation in my blood cooled. The tension in my spine unknotted. Music was cranked, the cool wind blowing through the windows, and my foot on the accelerator as I left Braxton Harbor in the rearview mirror. I didn't run away. Didn't think I was now. Just —this damn urge to see her. I trusted my instincts. When I ignored my gut, bad shit happened.

With every mile I put on the car, I relaxed more. This was the right call. The guys would be fine for a few days. They could handle it. If they didn't—well, I'd deal with it when I got back. The drive took just under two days, a little over thirty-seven hours, including a four-hour nap I took in the car at a rest stop.

I made it to Orlando in time to see her walking into the hotel. It was pure luck that I guessed the right one. Well, luck and the fact I knew their troupe had used that hotel before. She looked dead on her feet. The bitch walking with her looked like a bitch. I didn't know who the cunt was—wait—yes, I did. The chaperone. Okay, maybe a chaperone should look like someone smashed her face with a brick to create that expression.

Still...not a fan.

I followed them inside and made a show of checking the wall with all its pamphlets of local attractions while they checked in. Ivy looked so damn tired, but then it was still early and they'd been traveling.

"Since the venue is tied up with the riggers," she said while they waited on the hotel desk clerk to sort out their rooms— multiple. So, Ivy had her own room. How—lonely. Then again, maybe she wanted privacy. Having grown up with the guys all sharing the same room most of the time, I craved personal space, although it could also be too damn quiet. "I'll just do stretches and use the gym here."

The chaperone nodded. "Do not go down to the gym without me."

Ivy rolled her eyes.

I bit back a smile. I swore she gave the woman a look that just radiated "bite me." Kind of bratty, but I appreciated it. Rules were there to chafe but also to protect. Or so Ms. Stephanie often reminded us. The rules were also there to be bent carefully with just the right amount of pressure.

Pre-law had given me a lot of insight on that one.

As soon as they had their rooms and keycards, I noted which floor and let them disappear into the elevators before I asked the clerk whether they had a room available. Unfortunately, my plans had been blown at the last minute, and the girl behind the desk blushed when I smiled at her.

I got a room on the same floor as Ivy, along with the clerk's phone number. Maybe I'd make this a vacation of my own. She said she'd be off the clock at three. Good to know. She also worked nights sometimes. Even better. The credit card I used wasn't the best idea, since it was for emergencies only. Then again, I'd make do for now.

Instead of going straight up to my room, I went out to move my car and grab a bag. The nightly hotel fee included parking—thank fuck. Even with Sarah Jane's discount, it was still pricey. On my way back through the lobby, I winked at her on my way past. Her smile grew and mine might have made an appearance as I stepped into the elevator.

Getting laid hadn't been the original plan, but what the hell. It was still really early. I was just stepping off the elevator when the battle axe said, "Stay in the room, order room service, and catch up on your assignments from the tutor. You have my number." Then she was bustling up the hall.

"Whatever," Ivy called after her, and the door slammed. I

sidestepped the woman as she got to the elevator. She was on the phone before the doors opened.

Our gazes met briefly as she said, "Yes, three days—it's about time I had a break from the brat." Her look practically screamed fuck off as she jabbed the elevator button and the doors closed behind her.

What. A. Bitch.

She was just leaving Ivy here? Alone?

Irritated as fuck, I made my way to my room, which was just up the hall from hers. I glanced at her door, probably staring a little too long. We weren't directly across from each other, more caddy cornered. But when I checked through the viewfinder, I could see her door.

Well, the desire to be here fueling my blood made sense. The cunt and I were going to have words. Closing my eyes, I took a deep breath. Violence needed to serve a purpose. Carelessness was one thing. The woman was a chaperone, not a caretaker. She probably saw nothing wrong with leaving Ivy secured in a hotel room.

She was almost twelve by her standards, with Emersyn's birthday the following week. Even if she didn't look much older than eight. I was here. Here I would fucking stay, the guard dog at the goddamn door.

Every time the elevator dinged, I got up to check the door. The first was room service. Ivy opened the door but didn't let the delivery person in. Simply asked them to leave the tray and she'd get it in a minute, like she needed to get dressed. At least the sound carried from the hall easily enough. The minute the elevator dinged that the guy was gone, she pulled the door open and wedged it with her foot.

Dressed in a t-shirt and shorts, and apparently having showered since her hair was wet, she looked even younger. She picked up the tray and grinned. Really grinned. The door closed before it occurred to me I should have taken a picture.

Fuck, I was creeping on my own sister. Shaking my head, I returned to the bed and dropped on it. I was a light sleeper. The doors opened and closed in the hall. The sounds of families passing by, running kids, murmuring parents, even the occasional crying baby. All of this registered, but none of it was Ivy or a door close to mine.

The sudden fierce knock on a door had me upright and across the room, before I'd even processed I was moving. A young girl stood outside Ivy's room. What the fuck? The door opened and Ivy stared out, her mouth fell open in shock.

"Lainey!" I hadn't heard that squeal in years. It catapulted me back as Ivy threw the door open. The girls gripped each other in a tight hug, all but dancing before Ivy dragged "Lainey" into the room. "What are you doing here?"

Whatever the answer was, the door closing cut it off. Fuck me.

Adrenaline flooded my system. After emptying my bladder, I splashed water on my face and brushed my teeth. Every hotel room came with its own coffee maker, so I brewed a cup. It tasted like ass, but caffeine was caffeine and I'd had way worse, honestly.

I'd barely downed two swallows when the door across the hall opened again. The girls were coming out. Ivy had put her hair up in a ponytail and wore sneakers. She also had a purse strung crosswise across her body. Where the hell were they going?

"I still can't believe you're here!" Ivy's excitement punctured my anger so deftly that I damn near forgot why I'd been annoyed.

"I'm so fucking grounded," the other girl said with a laugh. "Worth it."

Then arm in arm, they headed for the elevators.

Son of a bitch.

I stuffed my feet into shoes. I was still in jeans and a clean t-shirt. It would have to do. I snugged a baseball cap out of my duffle and shoved it on my head. Wallet in my back pocket, I downed the rest of the scalding coffee in one swallow and headed for the stairs. I made it to the lobby in time to see them spill out of the elevator in a mini-crowd of people. It didn't take them long to separate over to the concierge desk.

The two girls, both possessing an unnatural poise, kept breaking into giggles that had me grinning. Tickets to the parks purchased, they followed the concierge's directions to head out the doors. Why did the guy just sell them tickets? Then again, I hadn't heard exactly what they said to him.

I crossed to him and handed him the credit card. Fuck the cost. "One ticket to the parks."

"Hopper?"

"Whatever."

The guy opened his mouth to ask me another question and I just fixed him with a look. This wasn't a social call. "Of course, one moment." It took two, agonizingly long minutes. "Here you go, the hotel offers a shuttle to the—"

I didn't wait for him to finish that part. I'd already caught the bus idea. Relief swarmed me when I got outside and found the girls waiting with a group of others for the bus. It was easy enough to drift into the crowd. I surged on behind them, sunglasses keeping my eyes hidden. They sat together, still giggling, and as much as I wanted the seat right behind them, I took one a couple more rows back.

At the park entrance, the thronging crowds worried me, but they also provided camouflage. I was just another kid on his way to the park. I didn't have a bag, but I also didn't set off the metal detectors. I'd left my knife back in the room. And I hadn't brought a gun. To see Ivy? I didn't think I'd need one.

For the next few hours, I soaked up both the park and the girls' reactions to it. There was no artifice. They laughed. They played. They bought each other t-shirts. Ate ice cream. Rode the rides. I did actually manage to land in the same conveyance with them more than once. They never noticed me. They didn't pay attention to anyone. I even managed to get a picture or two when they found a couple of villains, including the wicked-looking chick from Alice in Wonderland.

They made no move to leave as the park segued into the evening. There was a huge Halloween party, and you needed a special ticket. Turned out I'd gotten one from the dick at the hotel. Go me. They trick-or-treated around the park, laughing and playing madly. When the parade came through, they were right at the edge of the curb. The darker it got, the closer I drifted.

By the time the fireworks lit up the sky, I'd forgotten about the driving need to be here and just enjoyed their pleasure at it all. Then it was closing time, and we were all leaving the parks. The lines to get back on the buses were long. Thankfully, it didn't look weird to be standing with them and about a thousand other people.

I didn't let anyone jostle them, and this time, I parked my ass right behind them on the bus. Maybe I was being selfish, but I'd already figured out this was a birthday present from Lainey to Ivy. I hadn't realized she had such a good friend. Stupid, right? Of course, she had friends. But she'd constantly been traveling the last three, going on four, years. I wondered if she had anything "normal" in her life.

They planned together laughing giggles about everything they would do back at the hotel—more food, then a movie, and a sleepover. No adults. Just them. Perfection.

Good, once they were tucked into their room, maybe I'd give Miss Sarah Jane a call and —

"Oh, you've got to be kidding me." The snarl in Lainey's voice snapped me out of my plans and I narrowed my eyes at the two men standing between the girls and the hotel door. They weren't small, but they were pissed. Ivy was already cutting in front of Lainey like she was going to take them on.

Fuck that—

"Ignore him," Lainey ordered.

"Who is he?" Damn good question, Ivy.

One of the pair glared at Ivy briefly, before transferring that look to Lainey. Personally, I was about to pluck his fucking eyes from his head. *"Do you have any idea how long it took me to find you?"*

"Not long enough," Lainey told him. *"And this is my mother's lover's son, or as I like to refer to him, the human version of period cramps."*

The guy behind him burst out laughing and Mr. Period Cramps glowered. My lips twitched, because that was a damn good nickname. In fact, little Miss Magpie there just started forward like she was going to plow through.

"If you wanted to come see your friend," Crampy said finally. *"You should have just said something."*

"Adam... I don't have to tell you anything. ....let me be clear, you're like a cloud. A big, dark, ugly storm cloud and when you go away, it's a beautiful day. So, buh-bye." Lainey's voice kept dropping like she was fighting for the poise they'd abandoned all day.

Awareness of the pair kept my muscles coiled. I was gonna draw attention just standing here staring, though I sure as fuck wasn't leaving them behind. The girls almost reached his laughing friend when Adam whatever the fuck said, *"We came all this way, and we're not leaving until your ass is in the car with us and on the way back to school."*

"Sorry, my ass doesn't detach—unlike your personality.

Maybe you should put a bag over it or something." With that, she stormed past them, Ivy in tow. The pair shadowed them all the way to the elevator, and I was right behind them.

"Six in the morning," he ordered. "Meet us down here, and don't try to sneak off somewhere."

"Six?" Lainey snorted. "Too bad your brains don't match your looks. I'll be down by ten." She waited until the elevator doors almost closed and for a split second her gaze locked on mine and then she added, "Maybe."

As one, the pair pivoted to face me.

"What the hell do you think you're looking at?" the laughing man asked.

"Good question, been trying to figure out why two jackasses are harassing little girls. Only pervs do that."

"What the fuck did you just say?" Adam, the period cramp, demanded.

"I said," I stated as I stepped right up to him. "Only pervs harass little girls."

"Dude, you're asking to die," his friend warned, but I ignored the laughing idiot and kept my gaze on the guy right in front of me. Anger rolled off him like a storm.

"Go send them a cake," Adam ordered. "Tell them they don't eat enough. You—outside."

I chuckled. "Oh, what's the matter, big boy? Did I wound your pride?"

"Adam—"

"Fuck off and do what I said." Then Adam went back to glaring at me.

It'd been a while, yet this was a nice place—with cameras—so I just stepped to the side and motioned for him to take the lead. No way was I giving either of these assholes my back. Adam McDouche tried to shoulder-check me and missed. His friend groaned, but he cut away from both of us toward the hotel desk. I followed Adam right out the doors.

He didn't slow until we were on the far side of the building and half in the shadows. I expected the next move and avoided the hard drive of his right fist. His left came up damn near as fast and I took a glancing blow from that. The dick had moves.

So did I.

A hard uppercut slammed his teeth together. I took the next blow on the shoulder and the kidney shot that followed it, but he took an elbow to the face for his trouble. Blood sprayed the pavement and the scent of copper filled the air. More familiar than mother's milk at this point. His fierce expression showed zero signs of giving up.

Our next clash was just bare-boned bashing. Fuck, I took one shot to the eye that was gonna sting like a bitch, but the clap I delivered to his ear sent him staggering. The swift flow of feet was my warning that his buddy had arrived and I barely moved my head in time to avoid the fist he would have caught me with. As it was, it slammed him into his friend.

And I laughed.

They went down like some bad physical comedy.

When they got up, they were pissed.

"Come on, pretty boys," I told them. "Let's see if you can take me two-on-one."

The laughing idiot charged me like a freight train. I took the blows, blocking a couple, and then had to fend off Adam as well. It was like fighting the twins, only without the coordination. When I head-butted his friend, I saw stars for a split second, then Adam caught me in the jaw and I stumbled backwards, falling over a goddamn curb.

I rolled, managed to not hit my head or leave myself to get curb stomped when there was suddenly a little girl between them and me.

"What are you doing?" Lainey shrieked.

Fuck.

I backed off, panting, and shot a look around for Ivy. But only Lainey.

"Get your ass back in the hotel," Adam growled at her, but like me, he kept his distance. Even the idiot had slowed down. We were all bleeding and bruised. I hurt, but they would be hurting worse, even if I could barely see out of my right eye.

"No."

Arms folded, Lainey glared up at him.

"Excuse me?" he growled at her and took a step forward, and I went to meet him. At my motion, he froze. For one long second, we just glared at each other. If he took another move in her direction, I'd kill him.

His expression promised much the same.

"You heard me," Lainey yelled at him. "Have you lost your mind? Fighting out here? Why are you guys beating this guy up? Do you want to get arrested? Cause if you want that, I'll call the cops. Right. Now."

The laughing idiot started laughing—again. "Fuck me, Lainey, don't be such a little bitch."

Adam swung around, only this time, his fist slammed into his friend and knocked the asshole down. He didn't say a word to him, just looked at me then at Lainey.

"Fine. Get back in the hotel," he said.

"Not without you two. I apparently can't trust you and I also came down to thank you for Emersyn's cake. I was going to actually ask if you wanted to join us, but you're not going up there all bloody and gross."

A half-laugh escaped me.

That snagged the angry bird's attention, and she glared at me. "I don't know who you are or where you came from, but now it's time for you to go—while I have them distracted." She paused. "Oh my god, what did you do to his pretty face?"

Adam snarled when she would have taken a step toward me, halting her in place. Smart man didn't touch her, though. "Lainey. On the count of three, if you aren't moving in the direction of that hotel, I'm throwing your ass in our car and going home. One..."

She made a face. "Jerk." Then shot me an apologetic look. "Sorry, I never get to see my best friend." Then she turned.

"Two."

"You really are period cramps," she snapped.

The asshole looked right at her, pulled out some bills from his wallet and tossed it at me. They fluttered into the wind and scattered around us. "For your trouble," he said, then looked at Lainey. "Now. Go."

She went, and he grabbed his friend, hauled him to his feet, and then said to me, "Don't ever let me see you again, Mister."

I chuckled. "Or what?"

He stared at me.

"And keep your money, dick. I'm not for sale."

With that, I walked away from them, awareness of their presence keeping me on alert. I made it back into a side door of the lobby, avoiding the main portion. Last thing I needed was cops coming after me. I made it back to my room, pausing only long enough to hear Lainey's laughter along with Ivy's, before I let myself in the room.

Fuck, my bruises had bruises. I stopped dead when I found Sarah Jane lying on my bed.

"Oh my god, are you all right?" She sat up, concern all over her face.

"Getting better," I told her and threw the security lock on the door.

CHAPTER

THREE

LAINEY

P retty Boy didn't rush back with my bag. In fact, I'd been sitting there in my own clothes when he returned. To be honest, putting on previously worn clothes was not ideal. Not wearing his clothing was far more important. Sitting around in a towel, while making a point, would have left me in a far less powerful position.

There was a small fridge in the corner. It didn't have much in it, but I helped myself to a sealed bottle of cold water. Food could wait. While sipping the water, I made my way around the room. The shelves contained textbooks, law books, books on art appreciation, and more than one on the world of dance. There were magazines too.

Most of them were three or more years old, yet I recognized a few. They had articles about Emersyn in them, and he'd marked some of the pages that had picture spreads.

Her brother.

It would almost be sweet if it weren't so damn sad. She

didn't know what to do with a brother, and I understood that. I'd just gotten one, and I could cheerfully strangle him. Then again, I didn't want Adam Reed for a sibling or step-sibling. I'd be happy if he were no one at all.

I'd finished half the water bottle when the sound of the locks tumbling attracted my attention. I'd cleaned off a section of the sofa and had settled in with a stack of magazines. A part of me wanted to see what he saw when he looked at them.

Always seek to understand your opponent, Grandfather would say. When you understand them, you discover what motivates them and what can be used as leverage. The door opened to let the brute with the pretty face in. He had takeout boxes and my bag.

The zipper on the bag wasn't closed entirely and was definitely a little lumpier than when I'd put it in the car. He dropped the bag three steps into the room before kicking the door closed. He also used the key on the deadbolt, locking us inside.

The smell of food drifting from the white plastic bag reminded me that it had been hours since I ate. The fact he brought food didn't automatically earn him any points, especially not with how long he'd kept me waiting.

"Do you have any food allergies?"

Glancing up from the magazine I'd been perusing, I gave him a once-over, then shrugged a shoulder. "No."

"Good." He dropped the bag of food on the coffee table in front of me. "Help yourself. I'm going to shower." Without a second glance in my direction, he headed for the bathroom. The door closed behind him.

The key he'd used on the door had gone back into the pocket of the jeans he'd been wearing. That meant the key went with him back into the bathroom.

Interesting.

I went back to the magazine, despite how my stomach performed calisthenics to get my attention. The sound of the shower running intruded, except I refused to concentrate on the idea of him naked in the shower. Yet all it took was telling myself I wouldn't imagine him to conjure up that very image.

Pretty Boy had always been pretty. Well, pretty enough. The last time—the only time—I'd seen him before, I'd been a lot younger and he'd been a lot leaner. At least, I didn't remember him as being especially thick-chested or as broad.

Course, what did I know?

He's not remotely afraid of Adam or Ezra.

Fair. I knew that.

He loves his sister.

Sister. *Damn, Em. I wish you were here right now. I have a hundred questions and would live in ignorance if I just had you to hug.*

The article I'd been reading lay open on my lap. There were photos of Em in there that were taken right after her thirteenth birthday. They'd been interviewing her about being one of the youngest, celebrated artists to work as a professional dancer and exhibitionist.

Every word of Em's just leapt off the page.

"…I love to dance. I'm only ever alive when I'm up there…"

"Always. I've always wanted to dance and to perform."

"…injuries are a part of the art. Pain, though, can be overcome…"

Tears burned in my eyes. I'd always known she kept her pain bottled and hidden. Every once in a while, it crept out like a black vapor released into the air. Those moments held so much pain and—

The door to the bathroom opened letting out the wet, steamy air carrying a woodsy scent. It was the shampoo, conditioner, and body wash he used. The all-in-one product painted a sense memory of a lumberjack in his flannel, cutting cords of wood in the snow.

One hundred percent, not my type.

"You haven't eaten yet?" The warm timbre of his far-too sexy-for-fucking-words voice sent chills over my skin.

I debated ignoring him, but rude was a weapon one could only wield once to great effect. Better to keep it in reserve. Nothing could have prepared me for the sight of him standing there in nothing but a towel, with droplets of water skating over his chest.

He used a second towel to rub over his hair and the motion made the muscles in his arms and chest flex. The dark ink of his tattoo sleeves seemed to dance with the way his muscles moved. Optical illusion? Or just pure...

Pretty Boy snapped his fingers.

Absolutely not an illusion, I looked back at my magazine even as heat swept through me. The back of my neck was so hot I wanted to check if I was too close to the fire. The only fire present was a too damn gorgeous man with the face of an angel and a body that made me want to sin.

Staring at the magazine page, the words blurred out even as I mentally retraced the path of the water droplets sliding over his bare chest. A drawer opened, and the rasp of fabric sliding on fabric sent other images to dance in my head.

I flipped the page a moment before the smell of his shampoo and body wash enveloped me. No matter how I might feign indifference, there was no ignoring his presence. He filled the room, the weight of him pressing down against me.

"I brought the food for you to eat," he said as if I were a child who needed that explained. "The magazine will be there."

Now, I was curious. "So the food won't be?" It came out a great deal huskier than I intended. It didn't help that I was still mentally road-mapping those water droplets. Keeping it cool, I twisted to meet his gaze.

Thankfully, he'd gotten dressed. The t-shirt looked like it had been spray painted on. Mainly since he had his arms folded. He was also wearing a pair of jeans, although I didn't look any lower than that, nope, I turned myself around and faced the bag again.

Magazine.

Right.

I glanced back at the page I hadn't been reading. He leaned over the sofa and my nerves sizzled in awareness. The whisper of his breath brushed my cheek. It took discipline to not flinch. However, revealing personal feelings in public had been conditioned out of me for years.

He plucked the magazine from my lap before he whispered, "You need to eat, Miss Benedict. Ivy would be upset if I weren't taking care of you."

Ivy? The desire to be obstinate melted at the information. Or maybe the fact he withdrew from my space let me catch my breath. It could be both.

"Her birth name is Ivy?" She'd told me the story, but I didn't think she'd told me her birth name. Maybe she did. The moment the message had come through from her had pretty much turned my world upside down in the best way.

"Ivy Hardigan," Pretty Boy offered up. "That was her

name when she was born. It's still her name, even if the Sharpes changed it."

Emersyn was a classier name, sure. But it was also her mother's maiden name. Emersyn Sharpe. A product of her family. The first time she told me that, she'd rolled her eyes.

"Family names can be currency." My name, Elaine, was for my grandmother. I was pretty sure my mother had chosen it to keep my grandfather from tossing her out on her ass. Not that he would have. Sure, he threatened and he blustered...

This wasn't about my family or me. I twisted off the bottle cap and took a long drink of the water.

"Well, I wouldn't know. I put value in people, not names." The reprimand seemed to hang there like a gauntlet he'd thrown down for me to pick up.

"It's sad that you have to explain that," I told him as I stood. Sitting there much longer with him hovering behind me was grating on my nerves. "Though, we most often attack in others what we dislike in ourselves."

Crossing to where he'd dropped my bag, I reclaimed it and carried it to the bed where I set it down to go through.

"What the hell is that supposed to mean?" He returned the magazine to the stack I'd taken it from and prowled toward me. "You think I put more value in names than I do people?"

"Interesting question." I checked just what I had packed. The speed with which I'd left hadn't given me much time. But I had at least a week's worth of clothes in here if I were careful. Not that I planned to dress up for much. "Do you?"

"Do I what?" He was practically standing on top of me.

"Value names and positions more than people?" I raised my brows as I returned to perusing the contents of my bag.

46

I didn't really need to go through it all, but he didn't like it when I stopped focusing on him. "It's nothing to be ashamed of. Most people do. Society's rules and all that."

It was the world I'd been born into. The world I navigated daily. The world I planned to take over someday, if I didn't just dump it all to go live like some bohemian in the Caribbean.

"I just told you I valued people more than names." He sounded almost incensed.

"Huh." I pulled out clean clothes to change into and pivoted to face him. "Here I thought you were trying to make a point."

I made it all of one step before he caught my arm and tugged me back. A truly troubled frown tightened his forehead as he stared at me.

"I don't give a damn about anyone's name..." He glared at me. No, he wasn't glaring. He was staring at me, studying me. Maybe trying to predict me? "Why would you think I do?"

"Because you do...your sister is Ivy. That name is important, yet she's never gone by that name." That much I knew for a fact. "To me, she is Emersyn. That's her name. So yes, the name is important to you."

He opened his mouth then closed it again, and I began to smile.

"I believe that's one point for me, Pretty Boy." I have no idea what possessed me to tap him on the nose with one finger. Nor what it ignited in him because one moment he was just staring daggers at me, and the next he'd dragged me into him and sealed his mouth to mine.

His hot lips massaged mine in both demand and coax. The touch was intoxicating, and the first swipe of his tongue had my fingers spasming as I let go of the clothes I'd claimed. I had no idea where they went, just that my hands were now on his chest and his hand was in my hair.

With a little tug, he tilted my head to the side as he pursued my tongue with relentless determination. A groan rolled up through me as I tried to balance, but he knocked everything out from under me.

One moment it was there, and the next it had been smashed to pieces, dashed against the fiery rocks of his kiss. Suddenly, he wrenched himself away and left me unbalanced enough that I just sat down on the bed.

Panting, he stared at me like I'd sprouted a second head. Or maybe that was me staring at him. My lips tingled and my heart raced. The way he'd thrust his tongue into my mouth had been more intoxicating than a whole bottle of wine.

"You need to eat," he said abruptly before reaching the door. It actually took him a minute to unlock it and then he was gone. The door closed and the locks tumbled into place behind him.

Touching two fingers to my lips, I let out a little shudder. I'd been playing with fire, and I'd definitely just gotten burned.

FOUR

MILO

The pound of my fists against the heavy bag couldn't drive the feel of kissing her out of my brain. No, the sensation of her sweet lips beneath mine had practically branded itself on my soul. I couldn't escape the memory of her taste or the way her tongue darted forward to meet my invasion.

All I'd wanted was *more*. For hours. Nothing had pushed that feeling or desire out of me.

I shouldn't have put a single fucking finger on her. Yet, there she was, acting utterly unruffled by her position. If anything, she seemed more amused than upset by her incarceration.

When I brought her the food and her bag, I'd also been plagued by more than a bit of guilt because it had been hours. At first, I just needed the distance to get my libido under control. Then Liam and Rome were leaving with Freddie; there were plans to make and trucks to pack.

The best thing we could do right now was to look like

everything was normal. By the time I realized how much time had passed, I felt like a complete asshole. So, I'd done a run to a high-end deli uptown, picked up the most perfect roast beef sandwiches, a couple of club sandwiches, and a pizza-stuffed sandwich that smelled as good as it tasted.

It wasn't until I was opening the door that it hit me. I had no idea if she could even eat what I brought her. Ivy had a sensitive stomach when she was little. They said she didn't like milk, or maybe she couldn't digest it then. But no, she seemed fine now.

Maybe it was the kind of milk?

Fuck, I slammed my fist against the heavy bag. I couldn't remember, but it didn't seem to matter.

Elaine...

Yeah, that name didn't fit her. Irritation scraped away inside my skin. Hadn't she just told me earlier that I valued names and not people?

God. Fucking. Damn. It.

"You planning on having hands left when you're done with that?" Kellan's voice barely penetrated the red haze clouding my vision. Lust? Anger?

Were they any different these days?

Kissing her had been a huge fucking mistake. The press of her slight weight against me had been far too fucking alluring.

Maybe what I needed to do was go get laid. The thought of just finding a woman to fuck Lainey out of my head was as unappealing as fucking a hole in a wall. The rhythmic slam of my fists echoed the violent beat of my heart.

Why the hell had I slid my hand into her fucking hair? It had been so soft and tangled around my fingers easily. The idea of gripping it while I powered into her was an image easily summoned.

"Fuck."

I paced away from the heavy bag and panted as I walked in a circle. We used to have the gym equipment inside, but the rebuild for Ivy's dance studio had evicted all of it out here. It was probably better, the colder air in the warehouse should help my temper.

Should.

"You listening to me now?"

"Fuck off, Kel," I said in between trying to get my breathing under control. I was off the goddamn chain everywhere. My temper. My dick. My lungs.

"I would," he said without an ounce of rancor. "Except we have a problem. I can't and won't ignore it. Just because you say something is going to happen, doesn't mean it is."

Jerking around, I glowered at one of my oldest friends. No one who wasn't a Vandal, who hadn't grown up the way we had, could possibly understand the bonds of loyalty that tied us together.

Darkness marked the beginning of all our stories, darkness and loss. But we'd found camaraderie, support, and friendship, and we'd cemented it all in blood, sweat, and tears.

"What do you want, Kel? I'm staying fucking here rather than going with Liam to get my sister back." That chafed. Not going after Ivy was anathema. At the same time, I thought she'd wanted to leave and now we knew she didn't. What the fuck did it mean?

"The girl."

"No."

"Milo…"

"I said fucking no. She's staying right where she is. It's safer for her and for everyone else if we keep her locked down."

Rubbing a hand over his face, Kellan gave me an impatient look. "She came here to help Sparrow. She took an awful risk getting in that car with Rome and Freddie, and she did it *for* Sparrow. Holding her prisoner is poor fucking recompense."

"Then I'll send her back." End of story. I eyed the heavy bag again, then just walked away. I'd wrapped my knuckles but it hadn't done much good. The white showed evidence of blood leaking through.

I'd probably split most of my knuckles open. Whatever. Despite having showered earlier, I'd need another one. Even my jeans were uncomfortable, but I ignored it all.

"Milo," Kellan said, stopping me before I even took another five steps. "You can't control her. She did us a favor—"

"I'll do what I need to," I told him without turning around. He was right about her having taken a terrible risk to help Ivy. She was precious to Ivy. I'd seen that myself all those years earlier when I set out to just lay eyes on my baby sister for her birthday.

I hated that she didn't know who I was, even as I took advantage of the anonymity to watch over her. She didn't need to know us until we were in a position to walk into her world.

Not something we'd ever easily achieve now. Well, not me, anyway. Prison had beaten and stripped away what ability to believe in dreams I had left. Dreams for other people? Sure.

For me?

Fuck that disappointment in the ass with a razor blade.

Glancing back at Kellan, I studied one of my oldest friends, then said, "You want to do things a different way. Fine. I won't fight you on that. Maybe it was my fault we ended up here and she left—or was in a position to be manipulated into leaving. I don't know." I hated myself, in any case. "But her friend? That's on me. I will protect her and I will handle it. You get Ivy back, and I'll take care of this."

He sighed, then raised his hands. "Do me a favor?"

"What?"

"Go easy on her and yourself."

Rather than lie to him, I just nodded. Easy would not get Lainey Benedict out the door. No, she was made from sterner stuff and seemed filled to the brim with willful mayhem.

Something we just did not need right now.

If ever...

I paused in the kitchen to down a bottle of water, before I stripped off the wraps and washed my hands in the sink. The torn open and split skin was definitely not pretty. But they were barely oozing once I finished cleaning up.

After tossing the wraps in the trash, I headed back upstairs. The clubhouse occupied a massive section of a much larger warehouse. We'd discussed it for months as we staked out the warehouse.

The moment we were in a position to buy it, we'd all wanted to sleep here, even when sleeping here wouldn't have been that comfortable. We'd added on over time, but for the first time in years, we all had a safe place.

A place where we could sleep without worry of someone attacking, where the only people who had access to us were each other—the guys we trusted. I forgot the locks were there most of the time. Most of the time. Other times, I needed to lock it. It had less to do with trust than with the sound of the locks engaging. Prison altered what sounds offered comfort. I didn't try to explain it.

I'd left her after the kiss, and I hadn't slept since. Probably why I'd needed to beat my hands bloody on the heavy bag. Didn't change anything, however. She still needed to go. This life wasn't what I wanted for Ivy, but she might be a little tougher than I imagined.

Her friend was an entirely different story, and Ivy would kill me if anything happened to her. Maybe I couldn't keep Ivy safe right now—and that thought scored marks through me—but I would damn well keep her friend safe.

Jamming the key in the lock, I turned it with a little bit of a sigh. The tumblers, as they rolled, clicked, and the release echoed through me. The lack of light in the room had me pausing to let the light come in from the hall.

I scanned the room from the sofa to my bed. I cut on a wall switch that turned on the runner lights above. They were low-wattage and kept it dim, but they pressed away the darkness. If she was sleeping, I should probably leave her alone.

The idea of her sleeping though, proved alluring. The food bag was open on the coffee table. All of the sandwiches were gone. I highly doubted she'd eaten all of them, but maybe she put the leftovers in the fridge.

My stomach cramped. I hadn't eaten at all after I left, nor had I eaten anything in the last several hours. Fine, I'd check on her then grab food and go eat. I could crash somewhere else.

That didn't sit well, either. I glanced at the sofa again as I locked up. Keeping it quiet, I made it across the room to the bed. She lay on her side, her dark hair all over my pillow and her slim figure tucked beneath the blankets.

My cock jerked at the image even as my lips tingled. Reaching out to brush a strand of hair from her face, I curled my fingers into my fist and pulled away without touching her.

Soft fingers feathered over my sore fist, and I jerked my gaze up to find her eyes were open. It was hard to read her expression in the dark, but she stared up at me. Probably wondering what the fuck I was doing.

"Coming to join me?" The sultry words were like a fist on my dick, squeezing until I swore my balls wanted to explode. "I would have waited up if I'd known you were going to come back at three in the morning."

Was that the time? I didn't drag my gaze off her to check. The light touch of her hand on mine kept me in place.

Sitting up with a long exhale that half-sounded like a sigh of pleasure, she moved up to her knees and we were almost nose to nose.

"You know…you left before I could really respond to you earlier." Everything about her appealed to me right now, from the tousle of her hair to how her eyes were half-lidded to the faint pout of her lips. Her voice? Fuck, I could probably come from her voice.

Fuck, this wasn't why I was here and at the same time? I wanted to know. "What did you want to respond to?"

She let go of my hand to put her light fingers against my chest. The fact sweat was drying on me and I probably didn't smell all that pleasant registered, but I didn't back off. Not when she leaned in. Not when her lips hovered dangerously close to mine.

"You kissed me," she whispered.

Yes, I had. "I did."

"Why?"

The question didn't register with what she was asking. "Why what?"

"Why did you kiss me?"

"I don't...I don't remember." Probably not my smoothest line. I knew why I'd fucking kissed her. I'd kissed her 'cause I'd wanted to shut that gorgeous mouth and I'd wanted to taste her.

"Hmm." She slid that gentle hand up to my nape, and at her tug, I obeyed the contact, and then her lips sealed against mine. The taste of her was right there, hints of peppermint from toothpaste and maybe some chocolate? Oh, did she find my—

"Do you remember now?" she asked against my lips.

"Yes," I promised, fighting a losing battle against dragging her to me for another kiss. I wanted to kiss her until we were both drunk with it.

"Good," she said, then pain exploded through me as she fisted my dick right through the jeans and twisted. I didn't move, as all the breath left my lungs. "Don't ever do it again without my invitation. I'm here for Emersyn, not you. If you want to drive me out of here, you'll need much better material, Pretty Boy."

With that, she released me and settled back on the bed, before drawing the covers up.

"Do turn out the lights when you catch your breath."

What the fuck just happened?

CHAPTER
FIVE

LAINEY

Three days. I'd been a prisoner for three days. Well, prisoner might be too strong a word. Then again, what else did you call it when you were locked in a room? Milo brought food, water, and coffee. He kept his little fridge stocked.

He'd even brought in yogurt, which amused me for some reason. Yes, I ate yogurt. However, he'd chosen a particularly expensive Greek brand, adding granola and fresh fruit so I could mix it in if I chose. That, and he never slept in the room. I'd actually started to wonder if he was sleeping at all.

Then I forced indifference. If he wasn't sleeping, not my problem. I didn't ask to be locked in this room. As it was, I had my phone and my gun.

They hadn't taken my purse or searched it. I'd made a point of relocating the gun a few times each day and kept it within reach. He had plenty of hiding spots in the room. I was pretty sure I'd found a gun cabinet in the dresser. It was located in a drawer beneath boxer shorts via a false, if locked, bottom.

A safe in the closet promised other hidden treasures, but it was the books collected throughout the room that held my attention. He read on an interesting, if eclectic, mix of topics. There were textbooks on public policy, politics, and law. Scattered amongst those tomes were books on etiquette, society, and history.

The history books fascinated me for an entirely different reason. These weren't just school history books so much as focused treatises, memoirs, and biographies of particular areas, including the Bay Ridge families—like mine—and the history of the area's growth and economic development.

Some seemed downright arcane. More than one looked like it had been written by a college student. Or maybe they were just papers he'd written himself? The level of education and *discipline* suggested by the materials, impressed me.

Impressed and worried. In one of the top drawers, I'd found photographs. Not a lot, just a handful featuring a young boy with far too dark and damaged eyes holding a baby with a toothless wonder of a smile and an open expression like I'd very rarely *ever* seen on her face.

For all that, I could question the idea of Emersyn just *happening* to meet her long-lost, heretofore unknown sibling—it was hard to question the photos. Or my own memories.

This was hardly the first time Pretty Boy had been in her life. That lent some weight to what she'd told me, even though she had been circumspect in her details regarding any of this. Always protecting me and trying to keep me out of the line of fire.

It was as infuriating as it was endearing. The world we came from didn't suffer fools or innocence lightly. In fact, it would sacrifice both, only the price for destroying innocence came much higher.

I could try to deny he was her brother, but that was Pretty Boy's face in those photos. Pretty Boy's eyes in that solemn, too-serious face that threatened to shatter my heart. All I wanted to do was drag them both close to me and shield them with everything I had.

A knock sounded on the door as I made my way back toward the sofa. Pausing, I waited for the sound of the locks releasing that announced his arrival as the door swung inward. Pretty Boy didn't look good. There were dark shadows beneath his eyes and a tightness to his mouth.

We hadn't seen much of each other since that last kiss. He kept his distance, and I hadn't tried to bridge it. Picking locks was going to be the very next skill I mastered. If I could find something to work as a screwdriver, I could get the hinges off the door...maybe.

Unlike all his other previous trips in here, he carried no food or drink. He said nothing straightaway, just stared at me. I folded my arms and raised my brows. If he wanted something, he'd have to damn well ask.

"I'm going to shower and change." The growl of his voice was downright intoxicating. I'd been around many suave men and not-so-suave men over the years. Dealt with my fair share of suitors who wanted to make an impression —or at least they tried before Adam or Ezra learned of them.

After?

Well, it wasn't all that unusual for them to just vanish after that—usually figuratively, but there had been one or two literal cases where those guys just never appeared again. Pretty Boy, though? He'd faced off against them when I'd been young enough to find it damn near heroic. No one ever told Adam no.

No one.

Pretty Boy? He'd told him to fuck off with a grin on his face. The fact that Ezra had been ready to leap into that fight also hadn't done a damn thing to alter Pretty Boy's amusement. Even at twelve, that ferociousness in the face of Adam's superiority and command? Pretty attractive.

Now?

The corners of my lips twitched. It was still fucking hot, but I was *not* telling him that.

"Well?" The note of demand ignited a fresh wave of heat. Yeah, he was too damn attractive. That was a threat that needed to be contained.

"Well, what, Pretty Boy?" I kept the daring arch to my brows.

Eyes narrowing, he gave me a solid visual once-over before he scowled. It was almost like I could *feel* him counting to ten. The speed at which I'd annoyed him by doing absolutely nothing amused me.

He released a long breath even as he flexed his hands. That impressive temper of his took some managing. I admired a man who could handle himself, and Pretty Boy might have buttons to push, but he kept those reactions of his firmly contained.

"I'm going to shower and change. If you have something sturdier to wear that will blend in, you can go out with me."

"Not dismissing the invitation," I said, releasing my more defensive posture to claim the water I'd been drinking. "Although to what end?"

A soft snort escaped him. "Are you asking me what it's going to cost you?"

"Nothing is free." I shrugged. It wasn't what you were owed, it was what you could negotiate.

With a slow shake of his head, he said, "Nothing. I'll let you out for a few hours. You can stretch your legs."

"And?" Because when something sounded too good to be true, it normally was.

Exasperation exploded out of him in a huff of breath as he glared. "And we can have a conversation about you going back to your life, where it will be safe for you."

Yep. Everything had a cost. "I'll allow the conversation," I told him. Didn't mean I'd agree to anything.

Surprise flickered across his face. "You will?"

"Yes," I told him, granting his request. "Go shower, I'll wait."

With that, I took a seat on the sofa and flipped open the latest book of his I'd discovered. This was all about the art of dance. The fact he spent so much time researching all of this stuff about his sister was downright sweet.

The man was a tapestry of contradictions. It took him almost five minutes of staring at me before he finally vanished into the bathroom. I wasn't sure if he thought I'd just randomly vanish or what, but I waited, ignoring the sound of the water and the instant images the sound conjured of water sluicing over him.

Right, drooling over Emersyn's brother was about as far from classy as I could get. At the same time...

I glanced toward the closed bathroom door. Damn, he was a beautiful man. The hostility crackling in the air around him just added to the attractiveness. Between Ezra and Adam, I'd always thought my issue was just proximity.

That was why their damage was so attractive. So what was my excuse with Pretty Boy?

No answer readily presented itself before he finished his shower and came out dressed in fresh clothes. I hadn't even noticed him take any inside. I'd gotten my purse ready when the water cut off.

"You're going to change, right?" The question caught me off guard.

"No," I told him, giving my jeans and turtleneck a dismissive wave. "This is as casual as I get, Pretty Boy. Take it or leave it."

The ankle boots were flats and offered me plenty of support. If I needed to move, I could.

"Fuck it," he said after a beat, then grimaced. But he didn't apologize.

Good.

When he opened the door for me, I hooked my purse over my shoulder and sailed out the door. Or I attempted to, at least. He caught the bag's strap with two fingers and tugged it right off my shoulder. He'd already set it down inside the room and closed the door before I could react.

The sound of the tumblers locking into place told me I wasn't getting the purse out of there. When I stared at him, he just returned the look blandly.

"You don't need your purse unless you're leaving."

I snorted. "Nice try."

He shrugged, then motioned for me to go ahead, and I rolled my eyes before marching ahead of him down the hall. Awareness of his nearness pursued me, but I didn't look back.

When we reached the bottom of the stairs, he took the lead, and I hardly got a good look at their living space. Nevertheless, I remembered it well enough from my first day that no one else was present and three of them were on their way to get Em.

"Have we heard from them?" I asked abruptly. We could resume our game, but three days could be an eternity in a facility like Pinetree.

"Yes," he said as he opened the exterior door and stepped down into the cold warehouse. I followed him out, studying him. "They're there, and Freddie is in. Now we wait."

Wait.

Ugh.

"I know," he said before I could even comment, our gazes clashing. The worry in his plain for everyone to see. "They will get her."

"You trust them that much?" It wasn't a challenge to his authority so much as I needed some assurances here. I'd been second-guessing my choices the last few days, and I needed to know that coming to them had been the right thing to do.

"Absolutely," he responded without hesitation. He led the way over to a black muscle car. It wasn't sleek or low-slung. It was heavy iron and tactical. I had a feeling it would growl a lot like the man who held the keys in his hands. "They will burn that place down to get her out if they have to." Then he captured my gaze as I put a hand on top of the open door. "Feel better knowing that?"

"Actually?" I didn't need to play or pretend regarding this issue. "Yes."

Once I was inside and buckling my seatbelt, he gave me another long look before closing the door and circling to the driver's seat. No sooner did he start the engine than the vibrations rocked through me.

Yes, his car indeed growled and my thighs clenched.

The smell of motor oil, dust, and leather cleaner hung in the air, but not for long. An outer door opened, and then we were accelerating out into the watery sunshine. It wasn't really bright, but after several days of artificial light, I squinted away from it.

The snap of something in front of me had me squinting to see the sunglasses he held out. They were mine. Thoughtful. I tucked them on, yet it still took me a minute to adjust.

Without music or comment, he just turned the car away from the waterfront area and headed down a long city block. When he pulled into a coffee place and the drive-thru, I was a little grateful.

Coffee had been nice, but this sounded like a damn treat. After we had our drinks, he drove us out onto the road and then we were on the highway.

"You have questions," he said without preamble. "We're alone. Feel free to ask."

"I was free to ask earlier," I pointed out, savoring the next sip of the frothy milk confection. It was a perfect white mocha with a hint of toffee nut.

"But you haven't," he said. "Though I admire the very thorough search of my room and appreciate the fact you put everything back."

I shrugged. "A girl needs hobbies, and there's no reason to trash your place." I let the yet just dangle out there unspoken.

His soft chuckle sent another shiver through me. "Mayhem, you're a handful."

"I beg your pardon?"

"In prison, people like you were dangerous because you were cunning. You say little, offer less, then wait to see what knots the others will tie themselves into trying to determine your intentions."

Prison.

"Maybe you should worry about your own and not mine," I told him. "I've been transparent with mine."

"Have you?"

The challenge wasn't his first. He'd been full of them when I arrived, but our little exchange of kisses had created a demilitarized zone between us. Might be time to cut down that barbed wire.

"Yes, I'm here about Emersyn. Not you. I don't care about your time in prison. Whether you were there or not doesn't concern me. What does, is how you decide to behave."

Though he hadn't asked, I added, "While I haven't cared for all of your behavior, you seem to be acting out of some primitive urge to protect me. Understand that I am allowing it because it allows me to stay where we will hear about Emersyn. If that changes, so will my cooperation."

Silence greeted my statement. It remained silent until I'd nearly finished my drink.

"You...are not at all like I expected."

"Irritating?" I tried not to smile. Defying expectations was important. You could only keep people on uneven ground for so long. At the moment, I had no idea where we were driving. It didn't seem particularly aimless nor purposeful, for that matter.

I didn't even know why we were out driving, except maybe he wanted to speak to me alone and changing the environment offered him some position of power.

Maybe.

"No," he said, a lie if I ever heard one. "Not exactly.

Though I am surprised someone as educated and genteel as you is at all comfortable around us."

"Educated and genteel do not equal weak or ill-prepared. Or at least they don't always. Just like money and status can't make you a "good person," it doesn't necessarily make you a bad one either."

His snort spoke volumes for his opinion.

"You don't have to agree. You're a decent enough person." I hesitated to say good. While I might agree he was, he hadn't earned that kind of compliment yet.

"I'm not a good person, not like you are."

Laughter escaped me, part disbelieving and part just flat-out amused. "I am not remotely a good person, I'm just very good at playing the game." Better than some realized.

"You love my sister," he countered, and I smirked as I set the empty cup down in the holder.

"So? You love her too. Loving her doesn't make me a good person. Just means I'm willing to get dirty to protect her." No matter what it costs.

CHAPTER
SIX

MILO

"Freddie's inside," Kellan said. "No word from him or Sparrow. Liam and Rome are on watch." His tone was dead even and almost too calm. The fact it had already taken a few days following her "disappearance" to get Freddie in place grated on me. Based on Jasper, Kellan, and Vaughn's behavior, I wasn't the only one.

Putting on a show was our job right now. Tracking down potential traitors in our midst, the people who had been hired to photograph us, and making sure all approaches to us had been sealed up was the task.

For them.

My job was to keep Mayhem safe. Despite her denial of being a good person, there was no way in Hell I was buying her statement. Maybe she was every bit the hard-ass she put on the airs of, but I'd seen the same kind of ferociousness in Ivy's eyes.

Mayhem was not Ivy. That was clear. Although she was also nothing like I expected. At all. The desire to kiss her again grew more intense with each day that passed since our last kiss. The unreasonable attraction had begun a borderline addiction.

I spent my free time with her. Admittedly, most of it was when she was asleep. I could slip in there to watch over her without enduring the sharp sting of her biting wit.

Then again, maybe I was becoming something of a masochist, because I craved those verbal eviscerations on an entirely different level. It wasn't just a demonstration of how intelligent she was, though that was definitely a turn-on. No, it was the ruthless, take-no-prisoners attitude that draped her like some cloak out of a fairy tale.

She was not the princess in the tower who needed to be rescued. No, my money was on her being the dragon in charge of guarding Ivy. That just made Mayhem so much fucking sexier to me.

Dammit.

"Milo," Kellan said, and I dragged my attention back to the kitchen, where we stood drinking coffee. There were dirty plates and bowls in the sink and a faint smell in the trash can. We hadn't really done more than stack the debris and dishes in here.

Downing the last of my coffee, I headed to the sink. Washing up gave me something else to focus on. Every single day Ivy spent in that facility scraped at me. Mayhem's violent concern had rubbed off on me. I could tell myself all I wanted, that Ivy going home had been her choice. The level of doubt her best friend cast, though, made me wonder what we were all missing.

Even more alarming, Mayhem seemed uncertain of the precise danger beyond there *was* danger. Enough that she remained here, only reminding me that she stayed because she was willing. The funny thing about her cooperation? I believed her. I doubted anyone could contain her if she didn't want to be somewhere.

I wouldn't lie to myself on this particular subject. I found that part of her personality downright exhilarating. She just didn't need to know that.

"Do what you have to," I told Kellan after a moment. While he hadn't asked about Mayhem, he was thinking about her. "I have her."

"That's what worries me," Kel admitted.

"Then stop." I cut a look at him. "Mayhem will be fine. You want to do things your way, I won't fight you on this. You're not going to fight me on her." Because I would fight, and until I flat-out said it, I hadn't recognized just how brutally true that was.

Eyebrows raised, Kel stared at me. The shock in his eyes was as tangible as the shock it mirrored inside me. We didn't fight. Not like this. I'd fought them, in particular Jasper, over finding that not only had they brought my sister here, but at least a couple of them had also started fucking her.

If I focused on that fact for too long, pissed-off didn't begin to describe it. So I let it go. She'd made her feelings on this subject clear. She wouldn't put up with me telling her who to care about or see.

Exhaling, I shook my head. "Let it go, Kel. Just let it go. Focus on getting Ivy back. Focus on looking after Vandals business. I'll keep Mayhem safe."

I didn't care what it took to get Ivy back, and I got the impression that Kel didn't care either. I'd meant what I said to Mayhem. If they had to burn it down, they would.

"Tell me if you need anything," Kel said, bumping my shoulder with a fist. It wasn't a request. I nodded.

"Will do." Relying on my brothers for help was something I'd always been able to do. Time in prison had sanded down some of the links between us. Nonetheless, they were some of the only people I could trust.

I just needed to trust them again.

Once I had the kitchen sink emptied, I headed upstairs. I'd taken Mayhem out on a couple of drives. More for me than for her, but I thought she liked them. She kept trying to take her purse, and I kept putting it back.

She had a gun in there, which I'd emptied the clip twice now. However, the gun made her more comfortable, so hopefully, she wouldn't reload it again. I didn't want to leave her without defenses, but I also didn't want her to accidentally shoot me when I came in, either.

Course, based on everything I'd learned about her over the last few days, I doubted it would be an accident.

I'd barely made it in the room before the sound of the shower registered. The bed had been made, and the room neatened up. Gradually, bit by bit, she'd begun to organize my books.

Should a woman's very thorough search of my personal space be so appealing? Probably not. But then, Mayhem wasn't just any woman. The books on the coffee table were books on social etiquette. I'd been collecting them for years. The circles that Ivy had been adopted into weren't exactly known for their uncouth behavior.

Crossing over to them, I picked up one of the first I'd ever purchased. Jasper had been so fucking amused, until I made him read it and then he'd been appalled. Liam laughed at both of us, but then he admitted his mother had given him several lessons in etiquette so...

Yeah.

Flipping the first book open, I stared at the post-it note

inside with the clean, crisp writing that had just a hint of fanciful flow to it.

This is such bullshit. Learn social etiquette like you would Sun Tzu's Art of War. Etiquette is armor. Politeness a weapon. All you have to know is when to wield it.

Amusement curved my lips. The second book had another note in it.

This is moderately more useful, particularly Chapters Fifteen through Nineteen. I highlighted a few pages that you should revisit.

More than a little curious, I flipped to chapter fifteen as my phone buzzed in my pocket. The chapter was titled Meritocracy. Pulling my phone out, I glanced at the screen.

Bay Ridge Royals have been identified as an investor in Cascade Palace. Membership confirmed for all known members, including one identified only as King. *Rumor only,* King *expected to appear in person Friday at the following coordinates. You'll need an invitation to get in.*

The source was pretty highly placed. Liam and I had cultivated a government resource because everyone filed tax papers of some kind. Whether they used their real business or names, a paper trail was a paper trail. Coordinates, not a name.

The location was outside of Whorehouse Creek. It was at least hundred and fifty miles east of our current location. Whorehouse Creek was a small, ramshackle town that had been abandoned sometime in the late 1890s when a new railroad line went through about thirty miles south.

Some of the settlers tried to make it work, but by the 1920s, it had basically become a ghost town. We'd been there a couple of times for shits and giggles.

Invitation.

So whatever event they were hosting was in Whore-house Creek. That didn't bode well.

"What's wrong?" Mayhem's voice drifted around me like one of those cartoon aromas designed to entice and summon. I pivoted to find her standing there in a long, oversized tunic that left those stunning legs of hers bare.

The shirt hid whether she was wearing panties or not, which was probably a good thing. The red flush to her skin from the heat of the shower and the damp hair lent an air of vulnerability to her.

"Nothing," I said. "I just need to figure out how to handle this." Liam would ordinarily run with this type of lead. This was the world he'd gotten himself into, he could handle it. But I wasn't pulling him from getting Ivy.

"How to handle what?" She moved to her bag, the movement captivating even if I tried to keep my focus on my phone.

"A lead," I said. "We've been trying to track down some-one. There's a chance they will be somewhere this week-end, except it requires an invitation. I'd normally just send Liam..." Well, I'd ask him, but there was no doubt in my mind that he would go.

"What do you need? What kind of invitation?"

"You can't help," I told her. The last place she needed to be was even more involved in things.

"Stop being such a baby," she retorted as she stepped into a pair of leggings and dragged them on. The act of putting on clothes should not be so appealing. One would think nudity would be more attractive, yet there was some-thing downright enticing watching all that gorgeous flesh disappear behind the black leggings. "Money opens a lot of doors, Pretty Boy. I have a lot of money."

I glared at her, but she didn't seem remotely chastened

by my expression. If anything, she grew more defiant. One hand on her hip, she returned my scowl.

"What. Do. You. Need." The fact she fired each word like a bullet from a gun demanded a response.

I needed to track down this asshole who'd set me up. The guy behind so many other attacks on us. I needed to find him and eliminate him. Then maybe Liam could just come home.

"Use me, Pretty Boy," she coaxed, like it was an invitation. "You know you want to."

I snorted. "No, Mayhem. I don't want to use you. Or your wealth."

"If all you see is money and status, then use it. I'm here until Emersyn is back safe and sound. Besides," she continued, folding her arms, "I'm bored."

The corner of my mouth kicked up as an involuntary laugh escaped. "You're bored?"

"Holy shit, you almost smiled and your face didn't crack. Be careful. I don't want you to hurt yourself." Laughter sparkled in her eyes, but then so did a dare. A dare and a demand.

The silken tone surrounding *"use me"* stroked eager fingers down my body and wrapped around my cock. That was not what she meant, but my body was definitely on board.

Still, the amusement was right there. "I see a lot more than money and power," I told her.

"But that doesn't tempt you to use me, does it?"

Oh, she was wrong about that. Nonetheless, a conversation we would be better off not having.

"Do you know anything about a Cascade Palace? Or any palace event, really."

Lips pursed, she shook her head. "Not exactly, but I

know someone who will know. Are you going to have a fit if I ask to use a phone?"

"Did someone take your phone from you?" For all that I was keeping her locked down, that was to protect her not to just hold her hostage.

"No, I left it with my car when the boys picked me up. If someone decided to track me, I didn't want to lead them to you."

Smart. Admiration rippled through me.

Very smart.

Closing out the messages, I handed her my phone.

"Trusting me, Pretty Boy?" There was a definite allure to her smile as she opened the phone and dialed a number. "Or trying to tempt me?"

There were no safe answers to those questions, so I just stared at her and waited.

She grinned as a voice sounded almost tiny on the other end when they answered. "Hey bitch," she said with a laugh. "Miss me?"

CHAPTER
SEVEN

LAINEY

Whorehouse Creek had a casino. The name of the small town in the middle of nowhere that barely existed—anything connected to an LLC of any kind at least rated a blip on the radar of time. The original town, incorporated in the eighteen hundreds, fell into disuse as time and amenities moved on and past it.

But the town itself, and the land itself, did not fall into the public domain. As businesses died off, failed, or were just flat-out abandoned, they and their buildings were purchased then added to the land deed.

"One company owns all of it?" Pretty Boy leaned over my shoulder. The nearness wreathed me in his woodsy scent. It tickled my nose invitingly, and I had to fight the urge to take a long, deep breath.

Didn't stop me from wanting to enjoy it. I shifted on the sofa so he could see the computer screen more clearly. Like the phone, I'd needed to borrow a laptop. Electronic conveniences were amazing, while also making incredible leashes.

"That would seem to be the case based on public record. On paper, Whorehouse Creek is *still* incorporated, bylaws indicate a private township, security is also provided by a private company with no public police force, and land deeds are filed and buried." It was all rather carefully constructed. Too carefully, with each line of inquiry dead-ending after a few steps. It was how the palace system worked, or so Tally explained.

"There is a casino," I pointed out. It closed in the early eighties, but it had been there.

"Your friend said that was the place, right?" He was still right there, the tickle of his breath on my skin despite the fact his attention was on my screen.

"Tally," I said absently. She'd come through for me, and then there had been almost no doubt. Her latest obsession was extreme sports, on and off book. When I told her I needed a name, I could practically feel her assessing gaze as if it were on me directly.

"Tell me you're not in trouble," she ordered, and the stiff tone gave me a lot more insight into where we needed to go. Tally loved to party, but she was so much more than her celebutante image. That said, she rarely let anyone see below the surface.

"I'm not," I promised her. *"This is for Em."*

Pretty Boy had given me a sharp look, but I ignored him. Tally wouldn't betray me or Em. She'd sooner cut off her own hair.

"Leave it with me," she said. *"I'll get you the name."*

She came through in record time. Now I studied the business structure, at least everything available for public record. The name hadn't netted me an invite yet.

"I'm going to need to borrow your phone again," I told Pretty Boy. He just handed it over wordlessly. "Thank you, also, if you want to sit next to me, I won't bite." And it would be so much better than him looming over me.

His soft snort teased me, or maybe it was the fingers he trailed over my hair before he circled to take a seat on my right.

Focus, Lainey, I ordered myself. Unlike Adam and Ezra, who kept me out of everything, Pretty Boy had agreed to let me help, but only if I followed his rules. So far, that had not been a problem.

Then again, it was almost always easier to ask for forgiveness than it was permission. I'd only ever memorized five phone numbers. This most recent one had been for Fletcher Reed, Adam's cousin. He'd given it to me after he put together the new identity packet for Emersyn.

"Memorize, kiddo. Don't save it in anything. I'll answer any call that comes in, but if I'm not free, just leave me a message and I'll call you back."

Dialing the number, I made a mental note to delete it from Pretty Boy's phone before giving it back—I had with Tally's—I hit the green call button and put the phone to my ear.

"Roadkill Cafe, you kill it, we grill it. How can I help you?" Fletcher's sardonic tone made me laugh. The man was never serious, and at the same time, it would be a mistake to think him a fool. He might not have Adam's moody delivery or his brooding stare, but Fletcher disarmed everyone by playing the fool.

Thankfully, he'd never treated me to his idiot persona. Then again, I wouldn't have treated him as one. He was genuinely nice to me. One should always treat sincerity like the gift it was. That and trust. He'd as of yet not revealed my requests to Adam, so I kept my fingers crossed he would be as quick to assist this time.

"Hey, Fletcher," I greeted him. "I wish this was a social call, but I need a favor."

A long, exaggerated sigh escaped him at my statement. "Well, as long as it doesn't actually involve me cooking, we can definitely work something out."

I laughed. "Nothing so prosaic as an actual roadkill meal."

"Thank fuck. What do you need, little cousin? Shall I fuck up Adam's medical records and have him get a series of shots for a venereal disease?"

The image his offer painted made me laugh. "Tempting."

"Right? Okay, good. I didn't want to torture my second-favorite cousin, but for you—my favorite? Name it."

Snorting, I shook my head. "I need help getting some invitations and identities that will pass a swift background check, but also let me and—"

I spared a look at Pretty Boy, who sat so close the heat from his skin seemed to shimmer in the air. It was radiant. He braced an arm on the back of the sofa behind me.

"And a friend," I continued after the brief pause, "to get in without alerting anyone to the fact we're the ones going in."

"Okay," Fletcher sounded thoughtful. "Color me intrigued. Where are we going?"

"Whorehouse Creek Casino." No amount of practice would help make the unattractive name less grimace-inducing.

Fletcher released a slow whistle. Adam's cousin didn't say anything right away, though the sound of keys tapping on the other end of the phone told me he was already working.

"Kiddo," he said, his sober tone a warning. "This is not a good crowd."

The description could be applied to any number who traveled in our circles.

"Not a good one at all. I'm going to get this set up and make sure you have reservations. Who is taking you into this place?"

I spared a look at Pretty Boy, eyebrows raised. He nodded once. "Emersyn's brother."

Dead silence greeted that response. Not even keys tapped.

"You verify this guy's story?" A careful way to ask me if I needed him to do a background check. "Just say the word and I'll take care of it." Or if I needed help.

"I'm good," I promised. "We can trust him. Then I can send you photos of both of us."

Another beat of pure quiet. Was he reconsidering his offer? The phone muffled for a moment, faint conversation audible, but only because I could make out voices, not the actual words.

"You know the routine," he said when he came back. "Upload the photos to the cloud server. I'll have everything couriered to a box for you—since you said Em, I'm assuming Braxton Harbor?"

"Yes, please." It would go to the same box I'd sent Emersyn to in order to claim money.

"I'll ensure we have all the usual provisions," Fletcher continued. That would take care of the luggage. "It will all be waiting for you. Now, is this fraternal relation to your bestie right there?"

Even before I gave him the affirmative, I knew what he wanted. "Yes, he is."

"Fantastic, please put him on the phone."

I could argue. If I put my foot down, there was a chance Fletcher would let me get away with it. However, at the moment, my primary goal was to get this information, and I didn't need his loyalty to Adam suddenly usurping this request.

"One moment." I held the phone to Pretty Boy who stared at it a beat before he took it.

"What?" The growled syllable edged in hostility probably wouldn't win friends, although it would undoubtedly influence people. "Why do you need my size?"

He cut a glance at me and I just gave him a patient look.

"Just mine and not hers?" Whatever Fletcher said in response to that earned a flat-eyed glare. "Fine..." He rattled off the numbers then took the phone from his ear to stare at the screen.

The call had ended, but I held my hand out for it. Pretty Boy passed it over without question, then seemed to frown when he realized. "Don't scowl," I told him as I lined up a shot of him. I green-screened out the area behind then snapped a couple of photos.

At least one of them was so stern it gave me shivers. It didn't matter if they were perfect. In fact, most identification photos were of terrible quality anyway.

I snapped a couple of selfies, then sent them all over to Fletcher's cloud server before I deleted the contact info and the sent email.

"Don't trust me?" Pretty Boy challenged, and I stood, because his nearness was making it difficult to breathe, much less think

I patted his cheek. Another mistake, because the heat of

his skin beneath my fingertips and the hint of stubble just added another layer to my already overexcited libido. I wanted to curl up and just rub his cheek, feel the rasp of it on my palm as well as against my own face while we kissed—

Cutting off that line of thought, I withdrew my hand and grinned at him. Better. "C'mon, Pretty Boy. We need to pack. Fletcher will have everything we need and we'll need to get on the road as soon as we have it."

Fletcher sent a message within four hours that everything was waiting for us. Pretty Boy's shocked, then speculative, response probably shouldn't have pleased me so much, but it did.

I packed light, mostly my own cosmetics and clothes for going and coming. While Pretty Boy seemed to seriously consider leaving me behind, he didn't. When we left, there was no one around inside their little clubhouse and virtually no one outside in the warehouse either.

Did he wait for times when no one would observe us, or were they genuinely that busy? A question for another day. The drive took almost three hours and change *after* we'd picked up the IDs, the cash, and the credit cards. Everything would work, and nothing would be traced back to us.

Bless Fletcher, he'd sent a couple of different sets for both of us. I was going to owe him some lemon pound cake from Alethia. My grandfather's housekeeper made the absolute best, and it was one of Fletcher's favorites.

Despite being located in what was essentially an abandoned backwater ghost town, the casino itself was quite busy when we arrived. The casino and the attached hotel. I had Pretty Boy pull right up front and made sure he had cash to hand off for a tip.

Check-in went smoothly, but then I had zero doubt

about Fletcher's capabilities. I made a point of flipping through the welcome booklet they'd given us at the desk.

"Oh, look!" I gave Pretty Boy a playful, if not frivolous, grin. "They have a *spa*. I might go get all pampered while you play."

The bellhop taking us up gave me an indulgent smile as he flicked his gaze over me. Men were so predictable. They were going to look at my body anyway, so the empty-headed comments and smiles were all a distraction.

A useful one, but still a distraction.

I wasn't the only one who noticed, in any case. Pretty Boy slammed a hand against the open elevator doors when we arrived at our floor. "I'll take the luggage," he informed our escort and glared at him.

My body clenched at the heated threat in Pretty Boy's voice. The limited view afforded by the mirror in the hall gave me a good look at the bellhop's face, but not Pretty Boy's.

Yeah, the fact his threat caused sudden pallor and sweat was hawt as fuck.

"I need a bath," I said airily over my shoulder as I strolled down the hall.

"I'm right behind you." Yes, we were playing roles but damn if that didn't make my stomach tighten and a shiver scale my spine.

As promised, he was there by the time we reached the door. It was at the far end of the hall, nearest the stairwell. Normally, I'd object to being so far from the elevator. However, this also gave us another quick escape route, so I'd take it.

The suite Fletcher booked for us was fairly large, but there was only one bed.

Nice.

Shaking my head at it, I went to the closet; sure enough, there were already clothes waiting.

"What the hell is that?" Pretty Boy demanded, and I turned to find him glaring at the tuxedo hanging on one of the hooks on the wall.

"If you want to play in the big leagues, Pretty Boy," I told him as I drew my dress bag out of the closet. "You have to look the part. We have an hour before dinner is served. Get changed and give me twenty minutes." I paused. "Unless you need a shower too."

It was a calculated risk, but he just shook his head. Good. I took my cosmetics bag and the dress into the huge bathroom. I didn't linger under the shower, despite the luxurious appointments to the room.

I was ready in nineteen minutes, yet I took the time to inspect my appearance in the mirror. Anyone who really knew me would recognize me, but they'd have to know me well. Between the dress and the hairstyle, I was completely outside the bounds of my typical fashion.

When I opened the bathroom doors, I found Pretty Boy standing in the sitting room with a glass tumbler in his hand and dressed like James Bond in his tuxedo. Granted, the bow tie just hung loose, but he looked roguish as hell.

Whoever said the suit didn't make the man had never seen Pretty Boy in one. He was doing all kinds of sinful things to my thoughts on tuxedos.

His expression as I walked toward him with the loose red skirt flowing around my legs, offering the peek-a-boo effect to each of them through the various slits, was definitely a heady experience.

Heat burned in his eyes and I swore I could feel the flames licking me up. The bodice had a daring V that cut all the way to my navel. The silken fabric glided over my nipples like a caress, and the fabric tape would keep everything in place.

I felt beautiful when I put the dress on, so the desire flooding his expression was intoxicating in its own right.

"No," he said abruptly. The want vied with something far more raw and furious. "You are not whoring yourself out for this."

Hand on my hip, I snorted. "Don't flatter yourself, Pretty Boy. I'm window dressing. If they are all too busy imagining me out of this dress—like you are right now— they won't be watching you or how you're playing. Get your head in the game and take me to dinner. It's time to put on a show."

As I'd said, I knew how this game was played and I'd mastered a lot of moves over the years. This one? This was actually the easiest. Show the wealthy, the privileged, and the depraved a body all dressed up in an outfit that begged to be taken off and they were all going to be looking where we wanted them to be.

"Shall we?"

CHAPTER

EIGHT

MILO

I hated the dress the minute she walked out in it. The silk draped her like it had been painted on. At the same time, I wasn't sure even Rome's artistic talent could have done Mayhem justice. She looked like something out of the sexiest fairytale I could imagine.

Not Cinderella, because she certainly didn't need to find a prince or be rescued. No, she was like the good version of the Evil Queen or maybe the good witch. Either way, I wanted her out of the dress and not going down to a roomful of strangers who would admire her glorious curves.

Her walk across the room treated me to a sensuous promise of that silk gliding over her skin. How she managed to keep the strips over her breasts without even a hint of peek-a-boo killed and thrilled me.

"Come on, Pretty Boy," she invited, holding out one beautifully manicured hand. "Let's go find your guy."

Irritation vied with anticipation to scrape along the

inside of my skin. "He's not *my* guy." While not quite a snap, it came out a snarl.

"Yes, dear," she murmured, tapping my hand. "Give me your arm."

"Why?" Everything about this irked me. I did not want her going out looking so fucking edible. That dress begged to be peeled off, and I was going to be beating a lot of assholes senseless if they looked at her the wrong way.

"Okay," she said, lowering her arm and planting that offered hand on her hip. "Let's get this out of the way, Pretty Boy. You said finding this man was important. You didn't want to pull O'Connell from getting Em—a move I respect—so you need to do this yourself. We're here, like it or not, we're here. If your lead is right, then you get a chance to look at this person you've been hunting or who has been hunting you."

Reasonable as she made it sound, I didn't like using *her*.

"Now, currently, you're wrestling with the moralistic part of your conscience. Congratulations on still possessing that, by the way. But we're here. Both of us. I have every intention of helping you, and you can use my help. And if it turns out to be nothing, that the lead was wrong—well, what's the worst that happens, Pretty Boy? You spend an evening playing with me?"

Despite seeming to suggest the asking of a question, there was something far more playful that turned it into an invitation. An invitation I was far too eager to accept. From the tilt of her head to the curve of her lips, she exuded a kind of controlled competence.

"An evening with you isn't the problem, Mayhem," I told her. "If anything, an evening with you would be amazing."

It was the bald truth, and she deserved to hear it.

"The issue, though, is I don't know all the players in this game. We might not find anything. We might find everything. Worse... we might see nothing, but they see you with me and..." Too many people I cared about had been targets already.

"Aww, are you worried about me?" She dipped her chin almost shyly before closing the gap between us and reaching for my tie. "You don't have anything to worry about, Pretty Boy. I'm good at looking after myself." With a few careful movements, she set my tie and then smoothed down the jacket. "If there is trouble, you look more than capable of a scrap."

A chuckle shook free from me. "I'm not talking you out of this."

She clicked her tongue against her teeth. "Now, see, I knew you were smarter than you looked."

I rolled my eyes, but she patted my cheek, and I caught her hand before she could pull back. "Mayhem?"

"Pretty Boy?" I didn't care that she mocked the stone-sober seriousness of my tone.

"You stay with me out there. Nowhere alone. Nowhere I can't see you."

"That might prove problematic if I have to use the facilities. Nevertheless...I can live with that. It just means you need to be where I can keep an eye on you." Head back, she bared that throat to me like she wanted me to kiss it. Or maybe I was the one picturing kissing all that soft skin. "Shall we?"

Fuck. We were doing this. Turning, I tucked her hand into the crook of my arm. The gentle press of her right against my biceps was another reminder that we weren't just playing with fire, we were handling live incendiaries.

"Besides," Mayhem said as she glanced up at me.

"Pretty sure someone with your legal mind can talk us out of trouble, if necessary."

I snorted. She was going to be the death of me.

The trip to the hotel floor, following the indicated signs toward the casino, gave me a good look at the place. The clothes she'd had waiting for us were definitely well-planned. Everywhere I looked, men in suits and tuxedoes made themselves comfortable at tables alongside women dressed in the same type of finery that Mayhem sported.

Not that any of them looked like her, what few I'd glanced past. A host, a well-armed one, sporting a handgun in a shoulder holster that was hidden and a second in a hip holster that wasn't, stepped up as we arrived at the entrance of the doors to the casino.

"This is a private club," he said, his expression benign, though the blunted nose indicated a fair share of strikes in the past.

Mayhem released my arm long enough to reach into her little clutch purse. She pulled out what amounted to an electronic keycard. It was blank, with no marks indicating anything about it.

He took the card and scanned it with his phone. He glanced from it to her then to me before focusing on her again. "Good evening, Ms. Rushman. Is the gentleman your plus one?" He really did seem to struggle with taking his eyes off her.

"No," I informed him as I held up my own card.

"My apologies." The man was in his late thirties, easily. He had no business eyeing Mayhem like she was his next conquest.

It didn't help that she wore a Mona Lisa smile and actually ran her fingers over his hand when she took her card back. Then and only then did he scan my card.

Mayhem raised her eyebrows at me as though this proved her point.

"Mr. Noble," he said after scanning the card and glancing at me. Since Mayhem's worked fine, so should mine. Although his expression grew a little tense for a moment.

"I'm bored," Mayhem said, glancing up at me with playful eyes. "You promised we would have fun."

"I promised I would spank your ass and tie you to a bed too, if you kept it up." I had no idea where that came from, but it just rolled out and the corners of her lips curved even deeper.

"Well, I wouldn't be bored then."

The guard coughed. "My apologies, Mr. Noble. You are a VIP and should have been informed ahead of time. This is the standard entrance. If you'll both come with me, I'll escort you to the high rollers."

"Sounds like you'll have to indulge this boredom a little longer," I told Mayhem as I slid an arm around her. I didn't want her out of reach. The deeper we plunged into the casino, the more unusual it became.

There was a ring for fighting on the far side where a pair of competitors were currently beating the shit out of each other. Shouts came from outside the ring and at various tables. Our escort began to climb a circular staircase, and I allowed Mayhem to go a little ahead of me.

She paused at the next level, and it took me a moment to realize why. The sound of shouting and fighting below masked the fucking up here. Nothing could mask the smell, though. There was one woman not four feet from us swallowing a cock while two men pounded her pussy and her ass. She was giving hand jobs to two other men.

Beyond that little orgy were other beds and chairs.

Nude men and women alike danced, performed, or were getting railed.

I put my hand against Mayhem's lower back, and she shuddered. Worried, I locked onto her dilated eyes. Her nostrils flared as the woman getting fucked within an inch of her life let out a desperate moan before she choked on that dick.

Raising my eyebrows, I trailed a finger down her cheek to her throat, then along the gorgeous dip of skin to her breasts.

"Focus, Mayhem. We're not here for this."

Despite my soft tone, she jerked her head and blinked rapidly, as though just realizing she'd stopped. Another delicate shudder wracked her and she twisted away to start up the stairs again. Our escort waited patiently above, but he was staring right down at her breasts, or was until he peered past her to me.

I made no pretense of what I was imagining at the moment. I'd start by ripping out his eyeballs. They gave the first offense.

He backed up ahead of us hurriedly. Three levels up, he walked to a bank of elevators and scanned a card. "For the future," he said, finally taking his gaze off Mayhem and keeping it off her.

Smart man.

"You'll be able to use your card, Mr. Noble, to directly access these elevators. There's a skyway that you can use to cross from the hotel on this mezzanine level. Once inside, choose the top floor." The doors opened and he reached in to press the top floor as indicated.

I nodded but didn't say anything as he stepped back out. Then just before the doors closed, Mayhem gave him a little wave and a giggle.

"Stop it," I told her, and she laughed, a deep and throaty sound that made me want to smile even as I tried to scowl. "That's not stopping it."

"C'mon," she told me with a bump to my hip. "That was fun."

I exhaled and shook my head. I could give her grief about the orgy, but I probably shouldn't. Not when all I could think about was how easily that skirt of hers would move to the side and I could get a good grip on her hips.

The idea of fucking her out where everyone could see her but had no idea what I was doing exactly?

It appealed to me on a truly primitive level. Before I could linger too long on those thoughts, the elevator doors opened to a much more opulent level. Card games were being played and there were more people fucking, only they were behind glass and the sound of bodies grinding together was inaudible.

Mayhem shook her head as the concierge came to greet us. "Mr. Noble," he said. I didn't question that he knew who I was, considering the guard had used my card to summon the elevator. "Welcome to the Janus Club. We have set you up with a million-dollar line of credit per request. Would you like a second line for Ms. Rushman?"

"Please?" Mayhem said with a bat of her eyelashes, almost leaning forward into my arm as though to rub against me. The movement drew our greeter's attention, and I sighed.

"Yes," I snapped the single syllable and jerked the man's attention back to me. Mayhem was far too good at this and I was already on edge.

"Of course, do you have a preference for Texas Hold 'em or Five Card Stud tonight?"

I didn't care. Playing games was not why I was here, but

to stay up here and get a good look at all the others? Yeah...
"Lady's choice."

"Oh yay!" She gave a little clap as she bounced once, and I almost swallowed my tongue to laugh at the artless choice. It netted her the attention of every man in the vicinity.

An hour and several hands later, Mayhem did another raise. She hadn't changed a single card. She'd won more than she'd lost so far and played with an impressive poker face. She never looked at her cards more than once and seemed very good at flirting with every single man, even the woman, at the table.

The provocative behavior was going to drive me mad. I concentrated on my watered-down drink and tossed another chip in. I didn't fold.

Ever.

Nor did Mayhem. She pushed the other players, laughing almost as much when she lost as when she won. The huskiness of her voice and the way she glanced at me kept me on my toes. But it was the secrets housed in her eyes that made me want to go deep diving.

As it was, since she handled them so expertly, I had the time to scan the room beyond our table. I didn't know what I was looking for precisely, though we'd begun to build a profile of the man who called himself the king. No one jumped out.

Before long, an invitation arrived at the table. We'd won more than our share and had been invited into a higher-stakes game.

"Ms. Rushman may, of course, accompany you," the waiter said.

"Take care of these," I told the dealer, indicating our chips. They nodded as I held out an arm for Mayhem. As I guided her away from the table, more than a few guests stared after us. Our escort took us through a good chunk of this level. The private tables, the personal service.

There were dancers on the stages, all nude, and more than one writhing on a lap in the lounge areas. The smell of sex was flushed out with sweeter air blowing from above. Another set of doors opened into an even quieter room. There was a table populated by a number of unfamiliar people, but every single one of them wore a mantle of power.

They took their time assessing Mayhem and me. When I took my seat at the table, I tugged her down to sit on my lap. She might want to play distraction, but I wanted her where I could see her.

Chips were placed next to me, and the dealer gave me and then Mayhem a look. "Antes start at five thousand," she said.

I picked up the chip and set it forward, along with every other player at the table. With a nod, she began to deal the cards. Mayhem shifted against my lap and I kept a hand on her hip to balance her. Long as I was touching her, I could focus on the others present.

I spared my cards a single look. I didn't get the first bet, but when it was my turn, I tossed in the raise of ten thousand.

Which one of these pricks was the king?

CHAPTER
NINE

LAINEY

I t was after two in the morning when attrition during the high-stakes poker game took them from eight players to three. Despite spending the last five hours sitting on Pretty Boy's lap, all he'd done was adjust me from one thigh to the other. I had a feeling it was because of the erection he'd been sporting since he settled me here.

I didn't comment, and he didn't grind against me. Instead, I played my part. I flirted with the other players and shared speculative looks with the dealer—she was lovely and very professional. In and around me shifting against Pretty Boy, I also caught the attention of others in the room who lingered to either watch the game or move to quieter discussions away from us.

A part of me wanted to go and wander, but Pretty Boy's grip on me made it clear that he wanted me right here. A waste of resources, even as he played a mean game of poker and bluffed better than most of the other players.

But he had a tell. Subtle, though it was there. Whenever I caught a hint of it, I would shift in his lap and draw his attention. That wiped his tell out every single time. I never did the same thing, because otherwise it would draw attention to precisely what he needed them distracted from.

"Why don't we make this our last round?" the older man sitting to our left said. He was a big guy, with dark brown hair with hints of silver in it. Older than he looked? Or graying prematurely? He'd been drinking steadily all evening, but slowly.

In fact, I had to admire the way he let his ice melt to water down the alcohol. It always looked like he had a half-full glass and whenever he slammed the weak remnants, he ordered another immediately.

Pretty Boy's other opponent was slightly younger than our drinker but older than Pretty Boy or Adam. I would peg him somewhere around thirty. He had dark blond hair that looked brown. He wore a pair of tinted blue sunglasses even in here, not that it seemed to affect his visual acuity.

"Terms?" Unlike the drinker, he never asked for anything except a fresh water bottle, chilled and sealed. Paranoid and not afraid to hide it versus overconfident and covering with a socially "acceptable" bad habit that in turn provides camouflage.

Was either of these men Pretty Boy's target? I had no idea. He didn't give me any sign about any of the men we'd encountered or the single woman who had been involved in the game. She had folded the last hand and stepped away to have coffee and a cigarette, but she hadn't left the room.

I could see her in the mirror, still watching our game with a kind of detached curiosity. Then again, she probably didn't care who won as long as she didn't lose anymore.

"All in," the drinker said, giving me a look and then smiling when I met his gaze. "Add this beautiful creature, and I'll throw in another half million."

Sunglasses raised his eyebrows, but Pretty Boy went stiff. Considering the way they were playing, it might be worth the bet to test...

"No." Pretty Boy pushed the chair back and rose, setting me on my feet behind him, before he eyed the men at the table and the dealer. "She's not going into the pot for any amount of money. I'm out." He knocked his hand against the table. "Cash out the remaining chips." The remaining was more than three times what we started with; he'd hardly lost.

What the hell was he doing? But he didn't give me time to ask as he escorted me out of the room. The woman, with her snow-white hair and dignified air, smiled at me even as she raised her drink as though to toast.

Yeah, she could admire the caveman tendencies of Pretty Boy all she wanted. I was not impressed, yet I had to bite my tongue because I was the arm candy.

The doors opened below as he escorted me down the stairs and then we followed the route to the elevator we'd taken to get here. A man waited at the doors to the elevator, probably to keep anyone without a key from getting off.

"Do we need to go down to go back up?" Pretty Boy asked.

"No sir," he held out his hand. "If you'll give me your key."

Milo extended the card to him. He scanned it then checked his screen.

"Congratulations on a good night, sir. Your winnings will be fully funded within the hour to the account indicated. If you wish to play again tomorrow, you are welcome." He handed the card back then opened the elevator for us. "Ma'am, do you have a card?" He took mine and nodded. My more modest winnings didn't require congratulations or an invitation to return before he handed the card back.

"Good evening," he said, bracing the door open. Pretty Boy kept his grip on my arm firm as he stepped us inside. When I turned, one of the players from the table stood right there. The drinker who'd asked to add me to the pot. Pretty Boy cut off my view of him as he stepped in front of me and hit the floor for our room. Then three others as the door closed.

Silence crackled between us as I kept my temper fisted and my expression as placid as possible. No doubt existed within me that we were being observed. We'd been under the watchful eyes of cameras all evening.

When we got to our floor, I tolerated Pretty Boy's grip on my arm as he strode down the hall. I had to take two steps for every one of his, but I handled it. At least he wasn't dragging me or holding on so tight he might leave bruises.

As soon as we were in the suite, I stalked away from him and into the bathroom. My bladder was screaming and had been. It took me two minutes to find relief, then wash my hands, before I jerked the door open.

Pretty Boy stood in front of the windows in the darkened room overlooking the emptiness below. The lights here probably glowed for miles, yet nothing out there greeted our eyes.

"What the hell was that?" I asked, folding my arms.

"That was me not beating that son of a bitch to death for asking to purchase you," Pretty Boy stated in a cold tone. "He walked away with his limbs attached."

"You shouldn't have done that." The comment pulled him all the way around and he gaped at me.

"What the fuck?"

"You shouldn't have pulled out of the game. You were ahead of both of them," I continued, barely keeping my rising fury in place. "You had their tells, and they couldn't figure out yours—or at least they couldn't before you stomped out of there like some overbearing toddler taking your toy home."

"At no point am I going to bet your safety to a game of chance. That man wasn't interested in getting you a drink, Mayhem, or having you just sit in his lap for the rest of the evening. Every man there tonight wanted to fuck you."

I rolled my eyes. "That was the point."

If it were possible, Pretty Boy seemed even more furious. In the darkened room, with his back to the window and only a faint light from the bathroom, he looked cut from the night itself. "No," he practically snarled the word, grinding it between his teeth. "That was not the point."

"Yes, it was. You came here to find a target. Did it ever occur to you that it was him? You took your eyes off the prize. I'm no one in this game, which makes me an excellent weapon. Only now—those people are going to know I'm a point of leverage, and you just lost—"

Pretty Boy smothered the last few words when his mouth slammed against mine. The fierce possession in the kiss was an unrelenting demand. All the oxygen evacuated the room and my lungs as I fisted his shirt.

He'd shed the jacket somewhere, so there was nothing between me and the hard lines of his body except for the fine weave of his shirt and the silk of my dress. Heat licked a path over my skin as he devoured my mouth.

Flames burned through every tendril of thought. Push

him away? No, I wanted more. A button popped on his shirt. It struck my skin before bouncing somewhere else. Hot hands slid down my arms before Pretty Boy kissed a path from my mouth to my throat.

My thighs clenched, then one strap on the dress broke and it began to slide off. The lack of a bra became readily apparent as the cool air rushed against my nipples. They were already peaked and tightened almost painfully.

The sucking bite of his tongue and teeth on my throat made me gasp. I dragged a hand through his hair, pulling him closer as I arched upwards at the contact. The other strap snapped and then the dress just floated away.

Lifting his head, Pretty Boy stared down at me with wet lips and a dark expression that only sped up my breathing. He slid a hand down to my right breast, cupping it. The contact was almost feather-light, then he stroked his thumb over my nipple. I shuddered, but the sudden pinch was almost too much.

When I cried out, he swooped in and kissed me again, swallowing the sound as he alternated between massaging and torturing that nipple. I writhed under the contact as he kept me pressed up to him. The fabric of his shirt was a tease against my neglected breast and then his thigh was between my legs.

My panties were hardly a barrier to the way his muscles flexed against me. The motion encouraged my hips to sway and the pressure against my clit was pure ecstasy bordering on agony.

A minute later, he dragged me up and then I was falling. I hit the bed to stare up at him as he ripped off his tie and then the rest of the buttons on his shirt.

"If you don't want this," Pretty Boy said in a low, rough

voice that sent shivers straight to my pussy. I wanted to slide my hands into my panties and finish what he had started. I was a mess of want and need. "Tell me now, Mayhem."

His shirt hit the floor and his belt was next, followed by his pants. I hadn't even thought about what he was wearing or not under them. But the thickness of the erection, pointing heavy and fully straight, dried all the moisture from my mouth.

I swore the tip was almost discolored, it was so engorged. I knew what a cock was, and I was familiar enough with the concepts of sex to know where it went and how this was all going to end.

Licking my lips, I dragged my gaze upward to find him staring down at me. "I need the words, Mayhem. Yes or no?"

My pussy clenched at the emptiness. The heat rolling off him was like a hot desert wind blowing in the window. He retrieved his pants but didn't put them back on. Instead, he pulled out a couple of condoms.

Heart fisting at the thoughtfulness, I let my gaze rove over all the planes of his chest. His thick arms made me think of the way his thigh flexed between mine, which made me look down at his legs. The faint dusting of dark hair that spread down them and curled at the base of his dick.

"Yes," I said, the word slipping free as he tore open the condom.

"Put this on me." It was an order that I didn't hesitate to follow. I had to sit up and then go to my knees. I still had on my shoes, except when I reached for them, he said, "No, those stay on. Put the condom on me, Mayhem."

He cupped my neglected breast and began to tease that nipple much as he had the first. Fingers trembling, I slotted the condom over the tip of his cock. Moisture dripped onto my finger and I put it to my lips without thinking about it.

The immediate inhale dragged my gaze up to his as I let the bitter, salty flavor graze my tongue. His earlier anger and rage were still there but lust filled his expression as he stroked it over me, and I wanted to preen. Then he pinched my nipple so brutally that tears sparked in my eyes.

"You stopped putting the condom on," he said as though it were a warning. A ragged laugh broke from me. "The next time you want to taste me, it will be with my cock pounding between your lips. Do you understand?"

Delicious anticipation unfurled from the sharpness of the earlier pain. The discomfort bled into a river of passion and incandescent need. Thankfully, health classes had explained the application of a condom, so I got it rolled into place and as soon as I finished, I was on my back again.

He gripped my panties and tore them right down my legs. I'd never been so bare in my life. Even the thin strip of hair I kept from grooming seemed almost too much under the riot of want on his face.

"Later," he said, "I'm going to feast on that pussy until you scream and beg me for more."

My thighs reflexively squeezed, but he hooked his hands under my knees and kept them apart as he dragged me to the end of the bed.

"But right now, I'm going to fill that cunt with me, and you're going to take it, aren't you?"

Should all of this terrify me? It was so raw and primal. There were no soft kisses or stroking hands, just wild, demanding *need*.

"Do it, Pretty Boy," I told him. "Show me what you can do."

The first thrust split me in two. Fuck, it hurt. It hurt so much I nearly started crying as he sheathed himself fully in me. The pressure of his size and the hard push to seat himself shoved all the air out of my lungs. Tears spilled down my cheeks as I opened my mouth, even though no sound came out.

"Goddammit, Mayhem," he said in a raw voice, and I lifted watery eyes to gaze at his wavering face as he cupped my cheek with a hand turned so gentle, it encouraged the tears to spill out. "You should have told me." Then his mouth was on mine as he kept himself perfectly still.

The weight was incredible and too much. The teasing strokes of his tongue distracted me as he shifted, lifting away just a little before pushing back in. The pain splintered me, the discomfort easing a little faster this time as he kept kissing me. His hands were on my breasts, massaging and teasing, with no painful pinches.

Melting into a puddle, I wasn't quite ready for him to move, but he began to rock his hips and the pain flashed, then vanished faster with each thrust. I was stretched out so much, I didn't think it was possible to survive being impaled on him.

Nonetheless, he never stopped kissing me. He licked and nipped away my tears before taking my lips again, then he rolled onto his back and I sank down lower on him. The grind teased my clit and the first bolt of pleasure joined the pain.

Clenching my ass, I tried to move with him and then he guided his hands to my hips and pulled his head back. "Sit up, Mayhem...that's it, sit up and ride me. It'll be easier for you this way."

The hot and husky tone sent another pang of longing through me. As much as I wanted more kisses, the tease of pleasure had me chasing that, and I obeyed, sitting up so I could rock with him. He guided my hips at first, controlling the speed and the angle.

At my first gasp, when my clit got caught on a certain grind, he began to repeat that and then tears and light sparked as he dragged me down harder. The force made my breasts bounce and I tilted my head back as he pushed another cry out of me.

The pleasure overtook the pain and I writhed with him as he held me still, then pistoned into me from below. Every deep strike set off another firestorm of pleasure. Too much.

"Too much," I repeated, almost sobbing.

"You can take it," he told me, a grunt between each word as he increased his speed. "You can take me, Mayhem. Just let go..."

He might have said something else, but he slid two fingers against my clit and squeezed. My vision tunneled as pleasure pounded through me and then I was on my back, riding that dazed flow as he powered into me from above.

I clasped his shoulders as he pushed my legs up. Every thrust just dragged more sparks over my vision and then he let out a grunt as he shuddered.

Eventually, he collapsed against me, his face buried against my throat as we both panted for air. Sweat soaked us, but it was more than that...I ached from my head to my toes.

It hurt way more than I expected and felt better than I could have imagined.

Eventually, he lifted his head and stared down at me. Then without a word, he pulled out and off as he stood. I didn't know what to say as we gazed at each other. Then he saved me the worry by turning and walking away.

I slumped back on the bed and let out another shaky breath.

No regrets, I told myself. No matter what happened next.

No regrets.

MILO

After disposing of the condom, I splashed water on my face, then began soaking a washcloth. Blowing out a breath, I shoved the self-loathing back in the box. All night, the idea of sinking into her had been right there. It had been a wild burn in my system... the sweet torture of having her in my lap had been a tantalizing promise to myself.

Then some asshole wanted to add her to the pot like she was a trophy. What does she do as soon as we're back here? Demand to know why I didn't do it. Why didn't I treat her like a trophy?

Anger sizzled in my system. Mayhem... living up to her name, and fuck if she didn't look and feel every bit as fantastic as I imagined. Over the last few days, I'd imagined quite a bit.

Squeezing out the excess from the washcloth, I turned off the water and returned to the bedroom. I paused in the doorway as the object of my frustration and desire shifted uncomfortably on the bed. Her movements told me everything I needed to know about how tender she was.

I had not been gentle. Not until it was too late and she was already hurting.

"You should have told me," I said as I left the bathroom and stalked over to the bed. My dick gave a twitch at the sight of her turning on the bed toward me. As unabashed about her nudity right now as she had been the day she ripped off her towel, she lifted her gaze to meet mine.

"You wouldn't have touched me." The soft words damn near made me miss a step.

"Ease back," I told her, trying not to yell at her. She just had me—fuck, she had me—in that gorgeous pussy. She deserved a hell of a lot more than me spanking that ass of hers for not putting herself first. Stroking my hand up inside her leg, I didn't miss her trembling.

When I settled the cool cloth against her cunt, she grimaced and started to twist.

"No," I said, pinning her hip as carefully as I could without letting her get away. "It's sore and swollen. We just abused the hell out of you and made it do things it hasn't had to do before."

I kept my touch light but thorough as I cleaned her. The condom kept me from leaving cum all over her. Fuck, if that wasn't an image. I glanced down at the glistening folds that were violently pink in the low light.

My dick gave another twitch. I was already half-hard, and the last thing she needed was me pounding away inside of her, even if all I wanted to do was flip her over, lift that ass and fuck into her as hard and fast as I could.

"Are you angry at me because you wanted me? Because I was a virgin? Or because I was mad at you?"

Snorting, I shook my head. "I am more than capable of

being angry at you for all of the above. Except maybe the first one." A combination of pressure and the cool cloth was relaxing her.

The tension cording her thighs eased and they spread a little more readily. The redness around her nipples reminded me of how hard I'd pinched them.

"I'm not a gentle man," I told her.

"You don't hear me complaining," she retorted, but there was a hesitation in those too-confident eyes. "It hurt...but I always knew it would."

Refolding the washcloth so I could reapply it, I studied her.

"Look... Pretty Boy..."

"Do you have something against my name?"

She laughed, the sound was lyrical and looped golden chords around me. The last thing I should be doing was indulging this nearness, but she was very much a flame in my darkness. Incandescent and pure, with a kind of brilliance I thought you could only find when you flew too close to the sun.

It had burned me once. Burned me badly. What the fuck was I doing with her? Ivy's best friend and I—

"No, I think Milo is a lovely name." It definitely sounded lovely on her lips. "However, you've been Pretty Boy to me for years."

"You only met me the one time." I rerolled the washcloth again, pressing the colder side to her cunt, and she let out a little sigh. The line of her shoulders had relaxed and she leaned deeper into the pillows.

"What can I say?" She dipped her gaze, a hint of a smile softening her lips. "You made an impression."

It seemed a lifetime ago. "You took a risk going to see her."

"Well, arguably," she countered, pushing upward until we were almost nose to nose. "So did you." She raised her hand to touch my face, then hesitated.

"I won't bite."

"Ever?" The dare arrested me even as she feathered her fingers over my cheek. Using the washcloth had kept my direct contact with her light.

"Mayhem..."

"Do you have something against my name?" The parroting back of my own question pulled a real laugh out of me. I shook my head.

"No, I think Lainey is a beautiful name. Fits the beautiful woman who has it for her name..."

"But?" She traced her fingers up over my brow and down to my cheek again. When she brushed her fingertips to my throat, I tracked her gaze even as she continued to explore. Even these light, casual touches left a scorching trail in their wake.

"Nevertheless, you are mayhem," I told her with a smile as I finally pulled the washcloth from her cunt.

"So," she continued, running her fingers over my shoulder blades and then down to my pecs. "What I hear you saying is that I made an impression."

Laughter fell out of me at the unexpected comment. The way her lashes moved as she glanced up at me and her lips spread into a smile just captivated me further. I wanted to kiss those lips. What lipstick she'd worn earlier was gone. They flushed a deep pink and were swollen from my earlier kisses.

"You could say that." I could concede that much, like her, I ran my fingers over her skin. She was so soft. Soft, and curvy.

"I did say that," she teased and I shook my head. Then

those hot fingers of hers skated over my abdomen to my dick. Her thighs tightened as she slid her fingers around the base of my cock. Heat flashed through me and the semi I had been sporting thickened. "How are you feeling?"

"I should be asking you that." My fingers were getting closer and closer to her cunt. If I wanted to stop, now would be the time to do it. But she gave a slow pump up and down along my dick. The gentle back and forth was not enough to do more than tease, but it was a delicious tease.

"I asked first," she countered. "Although, because you've already had a bit of a shock..."

I squinted at her. Was she seriously giving me shit about *her* virginity?

"I'm sore, but it feels good too." Pride flooded me. "Real good, actually. I have to wonder how good it will feel when the pain isn't there. I've made myself orgasm before, but not like that."

The smell of her arousal perfumed the air around her. It didn't hurt that she smelled soft and perfect. The scent of her body spray reminded me of fields of flowers and sunny days. The most ridiculous of notions.

"How have you made yourself orgasm before?" Not the question I'd meant to ask, except she'd sparked my curiosity. Or maybe I just wanted to know more about her.

She squeezed the base of my cock, and the blood throbbing into it seemed to stiffen me even more. "Usually playing with my clit using my fingers. I got a toy a few years ago...a gag gift. It's a vibe and slender. I could wear it around my neck. Just when I used it..." The husky sigh at the end of the statement had my hips lifting to meet her stroke.

"It feels good," I assured her, even as I put my hand over hers. If we kept going... "As much as I would..."

"If you don't want to fuck me," Mayhem said with a kind of ease that baffled me. "Then say that. Even though I don't think it's a case of you not wanting me."

The words glued themselves to my tongue. I had nothing to offer her. When I thought it would just be a night to relieve ourselves after all the tension...

But that was before

Before I'd felt her come on my cock.

Before I'd thrust into her with so much force, it had *hurt.*

"I'm not a gentle guy." That was the problem. "Mayhem... Lainey... I spent three years in prison. A lot of it was in isolation. It was me, by myself, for twenty or more hours a day." The only relief I had was my hand and the idea of jacking off where anyone could hear?

Yeah. Fuck that.

Privacy was something I craved. It had been one of the first things I'd done when I'd gotten time to shower. I'd jerked off so much that first week, my dick had been sore.

But it was never enough.

"Am I your first since you got out?" The question held not even a single ounce of judgment. "Were you relatively a virgin?"

I laughed, really laughed, and shook my head. "Throwing my own words back at me."

"Only a little," she said with a careless little shrug. "You told me to say yes or no. I knew what I was saying yes to. Granted...your dick is the first one I've ever gotten to hold for any length of time."

A pulse went through me as she teased her thumb over my tip. The pre-cum beaded right up. Wait... "For any length of time?" The question came out on a growl.

"Hmm—yes, I'm afraid I have touched a dick before

yours, Pretty Boy. Don't be upset. Yours is very nice and so heavy... I guess I never thought about how heavy it would feel in my hand."

Her strokes grew more firm.

"Do you like it slower or faster?"

"I like it," I told her. "Depends on the moment."

"Earlier... you wanted fast."

I groaned as she traded hands then lifted the finger with a drop of pre-cum to her lips. When she sucked it off her skin, I wanted to come right then. Fuck.

When she'd done that earlier, it had damn near shattered my control and it was threatening to do the same now.

"Earlier," I told her gruffly as she shifted on the bed. "I needed to feel you...they wanted to try and win you like some fucking trophy. Your sweet ass had been against my dick all night..."

"And you wanted me." The wonder in her voice pulled me back to earth. "You wanted me...right? Not just some warm hole for you to fuck." She'd twisted around until she lay on her stomach and continued to stroke my dick.

Tell her it was a warm hole. Tell her. "It was always you." Fuck, Milo. Cut this shit off. But even as that part of myself argued against repeating the earlier experience, she laved her tongue over the tip of my cock and I groaned.

"You said the next time I wanted to taste you," she hummed a little sound as she lapped at my cockhead like it was her favorite treat. "It would be with your cock pounding between my lips."

"Mayhem," I warned.

"I don't know if I'll be any good at this," she whispered, the sound feathering over my dick. "But I want to feel your cock in my mouth, Pretty Boy, and I want to taste you. Then you said something about feasting on my pussy..."

The woman was going to drive me mad.

"I want you to taste me," were the last words she said before she sucked my cock right between her lips. Fuck. She didn't know how much pressure was too much or too little, but she had a steep learning curve.

When my cock hit the back of her throat, she gagged and then shifted. I followed her as she went to her knees in front of the bed. Glancing down at my cock resting on her tongue as she looked up at me with wet eyes, my control eroded.

"You really want me to fuck your mouth, Mayhem?"

She nodded, then I put her hand on my thigh.

"Pat me if you need me to stop. Nod if you understand."

This was absolutely the last thing I should be doing. I gathered her hair into my fist as she flattened her hands against my thighs.

"Relax," I told her. "As much as you can, let me control the rhythm and swallow with my thrusts..."

I waited for her nod and then gave a little experimental thrust. The feel of her throat as I edged it and she swallowed sent more liquid heat pounding through me. I kept them shallow, however, when she dug her nails in and my balls were dragging up, I pushed into her throat.

Holy fuck, her lips stroked my skin, her teeth grazed just enough to tease pain, and the way she swallowed. Too long without a lover, I was not going to last...

"I'm going to come," I warned her. "Are you going to swallow all of me?"

Tears leaked from the corners of her eyes, but she hadn't patted me to stop and I needed to know she was all right.

"I can paint you with my cum too, if you want..."

She tried to smile around my cock, then rubbed her tongue against the underside of it, tracing the vein. The orgasm struck violently as I jerked forward, pressing deeper into her throat. She gagged around me yet swallowed as I came.

I sagged back on the bed, pulling her off me and dragging her up so I could kiss her. The taste of me on her lips and in her mouth was a heady fucking combination.

I shut that little voice telling me this was a mistake up in the cage I'd had to keep myself in for so long. I shut the fucking door on it and focused on the woman below me.

Then I flipped her over and stared up at her. "Tonight, Mayhem," I promised her on a ragged breath. "We get tonight...now spread those legs. I need to taste you..."

ELEVEN

LAINEY

For some reason, I half-expected everything to go back to status quo when we returned to the clubhouse. We hadn't spoken about the man he was hunting or why. Only that he wasn't sure he was there.

Of course, when I asked him how he would know the person if he didn't know what they looked like, he said something I *wasn't* expecting.

"The man wants me dead," Pretty Boy said when we were in the car on the way back. "He's wanted me dead for a while. Pretty sure if I walk right in front of him, I'm gonna see that hatred for what it is."

That sounded nice, in theory, except... "If they've managed to keep their identity a secret for *years*, why would you think they *would* react?"

We lived in a world where the more skilled the liar, the fewer tells there were to even begin to interpret. Reacting to Milo's presence just seemed...

"Things slip," Pretty Boy argued. "Emotion complicates things."

"Not so much you can't be trained to avoid those slips." I turned sideways to study as much to ease the pressure on my pussy and ass as anything else. I was sore in all the right ways.

He shot me a narrow-eyed look. "It's hard to suppress an autonomic function, especially when it has something to do with a powerful emotion."

"Maybe. Not saying I agree, but why do you think this person must have a powerful emotion where you're concerned?" I wasn't trying to be a bitch, I genuinely wanted to know. It takes much effort to hate just one person. You're presuming that you are that one person for this figure. Only what if you aren't? What if you're one in a series of obstacles?"

His frown deepened.

I shrugged and shifted in the seat again, then glanced out the window. He'd woken me up by eating me out to the point I couldn't see straight, and then he'd pushed into me again. It was phenomenally better than the night before. Even then, I'd been sore afterward.

I could still feel the weight of him inside me, on me, all around me. It sent a shiver racing over my skin. If I licked my lips, I could taste him too. The things I'd done with Pretty Boy were all amazing things I'd heard about, read about, and *seen* in person, even if I'd never been allowed to participate.

The closest had been a guy named Pierce in my junior year. For four short, glorious weeks, we'd gone on three dates, regularly talked on the phone, and finally shared one intimate kiss that ended with his hand under my shirt.

Then the banes of existence barged in and I never saw Pierce again.

Adam had been downright incensed, but Ezra had stunned me with how he'd bodily hauled Pierce out of the bedroom at the Tarkington Estate. The party had been one I'd looked forward to because it was an escape from boarding school.

Of course, Ezra and Adam showed up to spoil my fun. Adam dragged me out of there and into his car. Then he'd driven me back to school. When I walked away, he caught me on the road and the next three days were made a thousand percent worse because they ultimately held me prisoner in a hotel.

Just thinking about their barbaric behavior and double standards could incense me. Their hateful attitudes and controlling behavior, however, had been a fact of our lives. Adam hadn't had a kind word to say to me since I was nine or ten. I didn't know what changed, but he went from thoughtful and considerate to a complete bastard and never turned back.

He was seven years older than me. I thought at first it was just being a teenager, but he grew worse as we grew older.

Before then...?

"I don't know what would be worse," Pretty Boy said, finally pulling me back to our conversation. "The idea that I'm just a number? That all this shit has happened to me, to Liam...because of being a statistic?"

I shook my head. "Hate can fight fire. Hate can fuel a battle. Apathy ends it. There is nothing more terrifying than bland indifference. It's the same amount of energy you devote to deciding whether you want Chinese or Thai. Neither type of food is crucial to your existence. Just the fact that it is food. You're an obstacle someone wants to remove. It doesn't mean you're anything more than a pothole rather than a speed bump."

"Jesus, Mayhem," Pretty Boy's frown darkened further as he glanced at me. "That's a cynical worldview for someone—"

"For someone what? A girl like me? A spoiled brat?" I dared him to take it to the conclusion.

"No, just...the ability to think anyone who would spend the kind of time and effort on killing a person, might be absolutely indifferent to that person and just to what they represent or block, is pretty damn disturbing."

He sounded so...honestly, troubled that I almost laughed. Almost. Maybe I was cynical. My world certainly didn't reward naïveté. The fact he could believe so much in other people's motivations?

I didn't quite know what to do with that.

"I have found that some of the coldest decisions are made when a person genuinely doesn't care about how the outcome affects someone else. Particularly if they see it only as a means to an end. The thing is, whether they win or lose, it's a statistic, a check mark. For you, it's your life... or your freedom."

He cut me a sharp look at that. I had to wonder, since he'd brought up prison a couple of times now. Was being in prison just another volley in their war?

After that, he said nothing else. I felt for him, I really did. Back at their place, he hustled me inside and away from the others. Though one of his friends—Kellan, maybe — I thought that was his name anyway, was waiting for him to talk.

In his room, alone for the first time since deciding to throw myself all into the crazy sexy times, I sank onto the sofa and blew out a breath. I genuinely did ache everywhere, though it was the best kind of soreness.

The violent awareness of his cock seemed permanently imprinted in my pussy. That, and the way his hands and mouth were on my breasts. Closing my eyes, I could taste the sharp bitterness on the back of my tongue and then feel his tongue as it traced my clit.

The last twenty-four hours had been insane. If I'd told myself even a week ago that I would be involved with Emersyn's mysterious, dark, and dangerous brother, I would have laughed.

Now, I couldn't fathom how I'd gone from there to here. The last thing I wanted to do was walk away or ignore the chemistry. Fuck the chemistry, I liked him. For all his blunt honesty and brutish chivalry, I found a great deal to admire about him. I wanted to know him more.

But I wasn't here for Pretty Boy. Or so I'd reminded both of us regularly. Despite having showered at the hotel, I decided to shower again. The hot water helped my muscles, washing my skin and hair, helped me get my chaotic thoughts, as well as hormones, in line.

I was feeling a little clearer when I left the shower. Only when I came into the bedroom, there was a very nude Milo waiting for me. He made no attempt to move or cover himself.

"Yes or no?" The sudden ferociousness seemed to have come out of nowhere.

"Is everything okay?" I asked, heading for him. Despite offering me every indication when we left the hotel that the sex that happened there wouldn't be repeated, he didn't look entirely so married to that idea at the moment. If anything, he seemed on edge. "What's happened?"

Hot scorching palms clamped onto my biceps. "Mayhem... I want to fuck you again. I want to get us both off. I just need to know, yes or no?"

A shudder worked through me. The heat between my thighs increased along with the ache. "I'm still a little sore."

"I'll be careful, Mayhem," he promised, then dipped his head as he fisted my damp hair. The soft caress of his lips on my throat, punctuated by the scrape of sharp teeth, reminded me of the dichotomy of silk-sheathed violence in his personality.

Pretty Boy was dangerous. Maybe to me more than anyone else, but not because he wanted to hurt me.

"And after...?" What was I asking? Did I even know?

He kissed a path up my throat to my mouth, and the first press of his lips to mine had me wrapping my arms around him as I let go of the towel. I didn't care about anything except the demand in his kiss and the feeling of him easing into me. The hot silken thrust of his skin against mine was already rocking me.

"You were sure of me," I told him in between biting kisses as he pressed me back against a wall, his hips rocking into mine with such precision the tension inside of me seemed to notch higher and higher.

"Why...do...you..." He grunted the words, his concentration fierce, and the vein throbbing in his forehead made me ache to run my tongue over the one under his dick. "Think...that?"

"You already had a condom on," I had to get the words out in a rush because he pulled out of me abruptly then turned me to face the wall.

"That was for both of us, Mayhem," he promised. "Hands on the wall and spread those legs....this is going to feel deeper, but it will feel good too. I promise."

I was already pressing my palms to the wall as he

dragged my ass back until it felt like I was on display, then he fitted into me again.

"Oh..." The word came out on a single groan as he began to thrust into me in a series of long strokes. He did feel longer, or deeper, definitely bigger. There was nothing I didn't feel about him in this position. The low growls he released in his grunts were charming as hell and stoked something almost primitive in me. "Pull my hair..."

I'd heard that... White edged my vision as he fisted my hair and yanked. The burn along my scalp was amazing, and his soft laughter as he began to pound into me with a kind of ruthless determination that threatened to drive me mad.

"Like that, do you, Mayhem?"

"Yes," I exhaled the syllable. I wasn't at all ready for him to tease my clit or for the force with which I came. It shook me all the way to my core. I could barely stay upright as he continued to thrust, the faint twists doing something exquisite to me and triggering spasms as I clamped down on him.

When he came with a shout, I grinned, almost triumphant and then he tugged me back to his chest and kissed me until I couldn't breathe.

Fifteen minutes later, I was screaming again as he buried his face in my pussy. I'd tried to be quiet, only he was relentless and every time I swallowed a scream, he amped the sensual torture.

It was heaven and hell. By the time he sank into me again, I didn't think I'd ever be able to move again. Thankfully, he carried me into the shower and helped to wash us both up before toweling us off and then when he tucked me into bed, he didn't leave.

He curled around me. It would be impossible to sleep

surrounded by that burning heat, except I drifted right off. When I woke to his erection in the morning, I decided to return fire with fire, and he woke up with me swallowing his erection.

When he came this time, I wanted to celebrate my triumph because he'd come with such a rush. We spent a lazy morning in bed after that. He only left for food around midday and was back soon later.

We talked. We fucked. We slept. But he never went far. Three days after we returned, his friend Kellan knocked on the door.

"What?" Pretty Boy called.

"They have her…"

TWELVE

MILO

"*They have her...*" Those words seemed to echo against the battered and scraped sides of my soul. It was another endless couple of days before we got word that they were on their way back. Mayhem, like me, was also restless. However, she seemed as intent on forgetting for short, intense bursts as I was.

I dodged the book that came sailing across the room to thud against the door next to my head. Woman had impressive aim. "I didn't say forever," I told her without glancing back before I unlocked the door. "Just not now."

"You're an asshole."

A pause at the door before I let myself out. "Yes, I am." With that, I locked her back in. My sister was out of Pine-tree. The twins and Freddie had her. They'd updated us the day they got her out, then followed up with far more cryptic notes.

Then the fuckers just stopped answering messages,

save for Rome. When I asked to talk to her, all he said was to wait.

So, I *waited*.

But I wasn't waiting patiently. Even standing in the warehouse with Kellan, Jasper, and Vaughn to go over what we knew about everything, I barely heard a word they said. My attention was firmly divided between the danger my sister had faced, my part in it, and the danger faced by the woman currently locked in my room.

Each day bled into the next. The agitation around all of us ramped higher with every hour. They were back in Braxton Harbor, but she wasn't back here... yet.

Liam messaged they would be here today *if* she was up for it.

If.

Keeping a tight-fisted grip on my temper had become a violent necessity. Mayhem had been more circumspect about the news. She's somewhere safe, she'd said. If she's safe, then we can wait.

While she wasn't wrong, I didn't want to wait. I wanted to see Ivy *now*. I needed to know she was all right. In the meanwhile, the guys discussed where we were on some of the missing trucks.

Only half-listening, my attention went to the external door rolling upward. The SUV pulling in had all of our attention. I could make out Freddie in the passenger seat with Liam behind the wheel. The engine cut off as the door rolled closed behind them.

The silence in the warehouse expanded like a rapidly filling balloon. The front doors opened, letting Freddie and Liam out. They left the SUV and crossed toward us.

I barely registered the exchange between the guys as I

kept my gaze fixed on the dark-tinted windows of the SUV's backseat.

I straightened as the back door opened. Ivy slid out slowly, her every movement almost ginger, as if she were hurting. Rome was right behind her. I wasn't the only one laser-focused in their direction.

The relief cutting through the tension let me take the first truly deep breath since she disappeared.

"Son of a bitch," Jasper swore before he strode away from us to scoop her up. Dropping my chin, I schooled my facial expressions. I needed to check all my own emotions at the door. The way she folded around him, and Jasper around her, told me a lot more about my baby sister's relationship with the guy who became my first best friend. The one I'd known the longest beyond Doc.

When Ivy had first disappeared while I was in prison, I'd been furious. Worse still, when I discovered *they*, my best friends, my gang, had taken her. Taken her, and at least two of them had seduced her.

I wanted her as far from this life as I could get her. Or I had... now?

I sighed as she trembled against Jasper, whispering the words "I'm sorry," over and over again. The desperation and loneliness in those words crushed me. Only when Jasper lifted his head from kissing her did Vaughn swoop in. He picked her right up and cradled her.

She seemed too small, too fragile next to his bulk, yet there was something electric about how she clung to him and he to her.

"Welcome home, Dove." His soft words carried then she was reaching for Kellan, and he took her right from Vaughn. Their kiss made me turn my head. I found Liam staring at me, pure defiance in his expression.

Like the others, he was ready to fight me. They all were. No more sending her away. No more taking them from her or her from them. The time to keep that distance had long since passed.

Kellan stroking the tears away from her face just crushed what was left of my heart. Sending her away had done exactly what I'd never wanted to do... it had hurt her.

The flash of panic across her face slashed deep grooves through my soul. Panic and mistrust. I'd cut her away from the people she cared about and who clearly cared about her.

I'd become the bad guy in her story.

Self-loathing crawled through me. With unsteady steps, she turned toward me and then, step by step, walked to me until only a couple of feet separated us.

"I'm back," she said. The lost notes in her voice threatened to gut me. "Don't make me go. Please."

I hated every choice I'd ever made that pushed her to this. "Come here, Ivy." I closed the distance between us even as she launched herself at me. I wrapped her up in my arms. My baby sister Ivy. For the rest of the world, she could be Emersyn Sharpe. But to me? She would always be Ivy. Always. "You don't have to go anywhere. I promise."

Always.

"You did good, Freddie," Jasper said as we headed for the clubhouse doors. I had Ivy tucked under my arm and she leaned into me, seeming for the first time to not be in a hurry to escape.

"I did *great*," Freddie corrected, thumping his chest. "Great."

"We know," Kellan said, almost patiently, and he glanced at me.

"You only think you know," Freddie said with a near flourish and winked at Ivy.

"Maybe, but I *do* know," Ivy said, meaning every single word. "You were my hero."

Coughing, Freddie actually glanced away from all of us, but Jasper gripped his shoulder. "Okay, hero, first coffee is on me. Let's go."

When Ivy would have followed them, I tugged her back to me. "Go on, guys, we'll be there."

She wasn't the only one who hesitated. Kellan actually pivoted and moved back to us, as did Liam. Both of them looked ready to throw down, right here and right now.

I sighed. "Guys, I'll bring her in. Just go. Give us a minute."

Kellan glanced from me to her. "You good with that, Sparrow?"

"Really, Kel?" I got it. They were pissed at me on a few different levels. But I wasn't about to hurt my sister.

"Yes, Milo," he answered without looking away from Ivy. "Really. We had this conversation. I thought I had made myself clear. Let me know if you need a refresher."

From anyone else? I'd probably have already belted him one. At the same time, he wasn't wrong.

"It's fine," Ivy said, finally. "Sorry, I'm still a little—tired." She reached out to take Kel's hand. "I want to talk to him, but I'm not running away. I promise."

Her statement went a lot further than mine, apparently. "Don't take long," he said in a low voice. "We have a lot of catching up to do."

Kel left us, but Liam still stood there, so I gave him a bland look. "Do you need to get her permission too?"

"Hey." Ivy jabbed her elbow into my gut. "That's rude, and Liam doesn't deserve that."

It irked me to admit, but... "Fine, you're right. Rude is wrong."

"Take it easy, Raptor, that looked particularly painful for you to say. Besides, I can handle you being a jackass. Just keep it in check with Hellspawn, or you and I will have a far more unpleasant conversation. Clear?" Not even an ounce of threat shifted Liam's pleasant tone, yet the pure menace in his eyes punctuated every single sentence.

"I'm not planning on being a jackass. Keep it up, though. We can solve this in a different way." I loved my brothers, but this shit was getting old.

Ivy cut between us, arms folded. "I don't want a fight."

"We're not gonna fight, Hellspawn," Liam said almost too easily. "Heading inside now, and going to be right on the other side of that door if you need me—"

"For fuck's sake, what the hell do you think I'm going to do to my own sister?" I demanded.

"Nothing," Liam told me with a smile. The genial expression never touched his eyes. "Because you know I'm not the only one who will kick your ass if you upset her again. We're not doing this your way anymore. Remember?"

"Thank you, Liam," Ivy told him just before he pressed a kiss to the top of her head.

"Yup. Right on the other side of the door." Then he finally left us. Asshole.

"Is this as weird for you as it is for me?" Ivy asked.

"Maybe," I admitted. "Probably should be awkward, and maybe this is gonna sound weirder still, Ivy—fuck, Emersyn."

"You can call me Ivy," she reassured me. In so many ways, she seemed almost a ghost of herself. She shouldn't have to reassure me. "That's the name you think of me as.

I'm your Ivy. I'm okay with that. I know I was a bitch to you—"

"You weren't a bitch to me, and if you were," I said, shaking my head, "I started it by being a raging asshole when you didn't deserve that."

"Well, yeah." Her easy agreement amused me.

"Tell me how you really feel."

"I think we did that once, and you were pretty insistent that you weren't a virgin." The droll comment made me laugh for real. Though, I had to admit to a bit of embarrassment considering who'd been sharing my bed for the last few days.

"Yeah, we're not going there again."

"Probably a good plan." She scuffed her shoes against the ground as if she needed to distract herself. "So, what did you want to talk to me about?"

"Nothing specific. I have questions, except you seem tired and I don't want to push you away by demanding a lot of answers." Which was one thousand percent the truth.

"I'd appreciate that." She should never have to thank me for being thoughtful.

"But—" I hated this next part. Just staring at the deep shadows beneath her eyes and the bruising in them. It would be impossible to miss. "—you've been through hell."

Shock danced over her face. Shock and a little bit of fear.

"None of them said anything." It pissed me off. I understood their desire to protect her. However, it pissed me off that they seemed compelled to protect her from *me*. "At least not the specifics of what happened this time. But my point is, you need to see someone, to talk to them. I want to be that person for you, even though I don't think I am."

I wanted to be that guy. I wanted to be her big brother,

yet it was about more than just her trusting me. It was about being less damaged than I was.

"Milo..."

"Nope, you don't have to make me feel better. This is one of the things that I should be doing as your big brother. Only we're not there yet." We'd get there. It was a goal. I liked having them. "That said, I want to take you to meet someone."

"I don't want to be sent anywhere..." Defiance flashed in her expression. "You said you wouldn't send me away."

"I'm not going to." I raised my hands, palms outward immediately. I needed her to trust me. That would take time. Right now, we had Ms. Stephanie, and she would be perfect for Ivy. She could listen in ways we didn't know or understand. "She lives here—in Braxton Harbor. She's a good person. Fuck that, she's a great person. The point is, she's been there for me. Hell, she's been there for all of us. I don't know a better person to confide in. She knows you— well, she knew you when you were little."

"Okay," she said slowly, not bothering to hide her relief, despite apprehension seeming a fixed point in her eyes. "Can I think about it? I'm not really big on strangers right now."

"That's fair," I said, then raked a hand over my head. "Are you—planning on staying here at the clubhouse?"

"Do you not want me to?"

Hands on my hips, I kept my temper on a very short leash. "It's not a call you want me to make."

"Wow. That truly did look painful for you to say." The hint of amusement curving her lips and definite spark of humor made me snort.

It was also funny. "It is painful for me to say. Do I need

to point out that you literally just kissed Jasper, Vaughn, *and* Kellan?"

"Nope. Pretty sure I was there for that part." I rolled my eyes at her patently unapologetic tone and sassier smile, even if she did shrug. "I'm not going to apologize for that."

"I didn't ask for an apology."

"Good." Except she sounded a bit tense.

"Apparently." Then again, so was I.

She sighed. "This is hard."

"Fuck yes, it is." I clasped the back of my neck. "Any chance you can just—go back to being someone who doesn't know anything about boys?"

The regret in her expression at least seemed genuine, if not amused. "Sorry."

"Right. I'm kidding—well, half-kidding." Tell her or show her? "Look, if I have a preference, I'd rather you stayed at Liam's place, or we get you a different place if you need to. We can come to you..."

"But you don't want me here."

"*Don't want* is a strong set of words." I was *worried* about her here. I'd probably be worried about her anywhere. "I just don't know if it's safe enough for you here. That said, I'm not going to order you to go back to Liam's or—anywhere else."

"You're getting better at saying those words." She almost sounded proud. What a little shit...

"Bite me." The grouchy comment slipped free and I glared up at the ceiling. "I'm trying."

"Yes," she said, barely swallowing her laughter. "You are, and I appreciate it. I don't mean to tease."

"No, teasing is fine." Better than fine. Little sisters were supposed to be annoying. I'd always pictured her getting away with murder because I would never let anything touch her. "It's actually kind of nice."

"Yeah? I've never had a sibling before."

"You can't tell," I promised her. "Just—can you think about it for me? As I said, if you want somewhere else, we can do that too. Not going to make you go anywhere."

"I can think about it." Although she wasn't making any promises. I got that.

"Thank you. Can I ask about the Sharpes?"

Her abrupt flinch set off alarms throughout my system,

"You really didn't want to go back to them."

She stared at me for a moment, then dragged her gaze away with a quick shake of her head. "We should probably go see the guys now."

She didn't want to talk about it.

"Yeah, about that—" I grimaced. "Before we go inside..."

"You just said you weren't going to ask me to go." Her defiance turned to real anger. She would never be shuttled aside again. Not without a damn good reason, and she'd probably fight every step of the way.

"I'm not. Just—there's something you need to know, and it would probably be easier to show you." Someone she needed to see.

"What?"

"Just—we had a little help in figuring out where you were." After that flinch, I needed to see her safe with Mayhem. Just to reassure myself, if nothing else.

"How?"

"C'mon," I said, gesturing to the door. Inside, Liam was waiting along with Kellan and the others. They made no pretense of having set up shop to give us time but were visibly ready for us to come in. "Really, guys? Subtle."

"Not trying to be subtle." Vaughn nodded to Ivy. "Actually, we were just talking about food, Dove."

"Save it for a minute," I asked, holding up my hand.

They shot me a look, but they didn't take long to figure it out. Ivy came with me as I headed upstairs then down the hall to my suite. The guys made a bit of a parade behind us. Pulling the keys from my pocket, I unlocked the door and pushed it open.

"Oh, you're back. Be still my heart…" Mayhem practically drawled. I could hear the fight edging each word, even as my attention stayed on Ivy.

"Lainey?"

A moment later, she rushed the room and collided with Mayhem, and they both burst into tears. Tears that set fire to my own eyes. I dipped my chin as I soaked up the way they clung to each other.

Now… she was home.

CHAPTER

THIRTEEN

LAINEY

My eyes were sore, irritated, and a little swollen. We'd shed more tears in the last few days than I had during the previous five years. I thought my loathing for her family could not grow more intense.

I was wrong.

Adam had always despised her family, particularly her uncle. Had he known? That thought settled into the back of my brain not long after she confessed to some of the horrors. Confessed to years of abuse suffered at her uncle's hands. Abuse Adam must have suspected because he asked Em to marry him.

That...I put that information away. I didn't quite know what to do with it at the moment. Em was the important one. She was hurting on so many levels. I'd sat with her for hours in her studio. Watched her work out. She hadn't been this shaky after we'd had to go to that woman's clinic.

I hated her uncle so much. The first thing I planned to do when I went home was speak to my grandfather. There were a lot of different ways to go after someone with the Sharpes' level of influence. Fortunately, I was a Benedict, and we had our own wealth and influence to wield as a weapon.

The days following Emersyn's return had been marked by time with her and time with Pretty Boy. He seemed so uncertain around her, which puzzled me at first. Em was a delight, tough as steel, but far more likely to smooth the way than cause drama or engage in a battle of personalities.

For his part, Pretty Boy genuinely didn't know what to do about her. It was like he floundered, out of his depth, where she was concerned. Of course, when Adam made an appearance at the clubhouse, Pretty Boy hauled me out of there before I even got to say two words to him.

Regret stabbed at me on that particular subject. At the same time, I wasn't even sure what to say to Adam at this point. With the exception of the nights I slept with Em, and Rome came in to sleep on her other side, I'd been in Pretty Boy's bed every night.

The sex was....better. The soreness was still there, but I didn't think I would ever get used to that steel iron he wielded in his dick. Not that I was complaining.

Much.

Emersyn had been curious, but then she'd also given me privacy. Watching the other guys with her, there was no mistaking the deep love and affection surrounding her. Honestly, I wasn't even sure why it was on my mind but sleep had been elusive most of the night.

"What's wrong?" Pretty Boy asked, the bristle from his stubble scraping over my shoulder. I'd been alone when I went to bed, and I hadn't noticed when he came in. At the same time, there was comfort in the way he folded around me.

That, and he always slept between me and the door. I didn't ask; it seemed to be something he required.

"Nothing," I said, more because I wasn't sure why I was worrying at the moment. He stroked a hand up over my chest to my head, and then he fisted my hair. The tug lit up my scalp, even as he rubbed his erection against my ass. Despite how turned-on he was and the liquid heat unfurling in me, he never took anything without asking.

Every. Single. Time.

"What do you need then?"

Oh, I shuddered as he mouthed kisses over my shoulder. Then he delved his free hand between my thighs. Tracing circles around my clit even as he locked a leg over mine so I couldn't go anywhere.

"That's nice," I exhaled on a shudder.

"Do you need nice?"

Did I?

I clenched my thighs around his hand. He worked one finger inside me even with my tightness and then he scraped his teeth over my pulse point as he controlled my head with his fist in my hair.

"Pretty Boy," I groaned. "I need you...hard and fast...like that first time."

It was all I had to say before he rolled me over onto my stomach and then my ass was in the air. I wasn't ready for his mouth to press up against my pussy or his tongue to invade. I was already soaked and he let out a groan that shivered through me.

Nonetheless, he didn't take any time straightening to line up his cock, and then he drove it in to me. I slammed my fist against the bed at how hot and hard he felt inside me.

"Yes?" He stilled, impaling me on that glorious cock with his hand flat against my back.

"Yes," I moaned. "All the yes...fuck me, Pretty Boy. I want to feel you for days."

Wanted to feel him even when I needed to go, because the clock on my time here was rapidly dwindling down. He took me at my word, his powerful thrusts shoved me up on the bed, even as his hands on my hips kept dragging me back to him.

I pulsed around him, my inner muscles desperate to clamp down on his thick cock.

"Fuck." The word rode a ragged breath out of him. "Your cunt is the hottest, sexiest fucking thing, Mayhem. I can feel you squeezing me. I never want to leave this cunt. I want to fill you over and over."

It was what I wanted too.

"Then there are these breasts. Your nipples are like beaded little raspberries, red and stiff. Almost as sweet as you, only so much better." The slap of his skin against mine just added another layer as he cupped my breasts and dragged me upward until my back was to his chest.

I tilted my head back, and then his mouth swooped down to claim my lips. The kiss tasted like fire. The stubble on his face scraped my cheeks. Everywhere we touched, I was on the edge between pleasure and pain, even in my pussy.

Maybe especially there. He was so big, his thrusts so hard, and then he seemed to strike that spot as he rubbed two callused fingers against my clit and I screamed into his mouth.

I bucked, it was too much. Far too much. Then he replaced his fingers with a little vibe, and I lost it. There was no controlling my reaction as I came. He kept stretching me out around him as he thrust until his own pace staggered, the uneven movements giving way to the hot jets of cum filling me.

We collapsed to the bed, panting together. It was the first time he came inside me without a condom. The thought registered as I kept spasming around him. He let out a little harsh exhale each time I squeezed him.

"I fucked up," he said with a groan.

"No," I told him, not letting him pull away. "That was perfect..."

"No condom." Yeah, I knew. The apology and worry in his voice had me twisting in his arms. It slipped his cock out of me and cum leaked out onto my thighs. That was messy, but right now I didn't care about that. I cared about him.

"Birth control is covered," I promised him. "I'm clean. I'm assuming you are, because you are far too controlled to have slipped like that if there was something you were guarding against."

Even in the dim light of the room, I could read the surprise on his face. "I'm clean." It was a promise.

"Then that was fine..." I nipped his lower lip. "Better than fine. It was fucking amazing. You have no idea how good you feel."

He grinned. "Are you still sore?"

"Not really. Want to get me there?"

I swore his cock twitched. He didn't answer me in words, instead, he flipped me onto my back and began to pepper my chest with kisses.

I had no idea how long we lingered in his room that day. I needed more time, but it wasn't meant to be. We had a day or two, time with Emersyn, and then Ezra was there. Em came to tell me and Pretty Boy was furious.

It looked like he wanted to forbid me from speaking to him, except that wasn't possible. Ezra and I went way back... Em had spoken to him, and she said he was really worried. Despite Pretty Boy's objections, I talked to Ezra alone. He was right outside and would be in their office in a flash if I needed him.

Walking into the office, with its worn walls and furniture, was like walking into a different world. Even stranger, coming face to face with Ezra there, was like waking up to a completely different one. I wasn't the girl I'd been when we last spoke.

The wild heat in his dark green eyes scorched me before they shuttered. He was shackled to the desk. I frowned at the restraints, but he gave me a once-over.

"What the fuck are you doing here, Lainey?" The lack of emotion in his voice wasn't anything new. Ezra had the ability to skin people alive with his anger, yet he usually saved his rancor with me for when he was drunk.

He didn't appear to be even tipsy at the moment. Folding my arms, I stared at him. "Why are *you* here?"

"I asked first," he snapped back, but there was a tiredness in Ezra Graham's voice that worried me. The intensity of his stare wasn't really helping. "You have no business being here or taking these kinds of risks—"

"I think I'll decide what risks I can and will take," I cut him off. "I'm here for Emersyn. I'm assuming that's why you're here."

He opened his mouth then snapped it shut again. He blew out an aggrieved breath. "I've been trying to find Adam."

"Well, he was here the other day," I told him with a shrug. "You should get them to take you to wherever he is."

"You didn't talk to him?" Shock stamped itself on his expression.

"No." I kept it simple, shrugging. "I told you, I'm here for Em. She needs me."

"Then get her, and let's take her back with us."

Yeah, that wasn't happening. Not that I wouldn't use every resource at my disposal to protect her, but Emersyn was invested in these guys. Then there was Pretty Boy.

"Go home, Ezra. When I'm done, and if I need a ride, I'll call." That was about all I could offer him.

"Andrea will be home soon." Of course, he'd bring up my younger sister. He cared about her too. She was also Adam's sister.

"I know, and I'll be there when she is back."

"You should leave now," he said, his hand flexing as he couldn't move from where he'd been shackled. "With me. This is the last place you should be, and if you don't think I won't come back here with enough people to take them—"

I raised a hand, and he stopped. "Ezra, they're Emersyn's family. You're going to leave them alone."

His eyes narrowed. "You have no idea what is going on..."

Pushing away from the wall, I crossed to where he stood. "I know a lot more than you think. Just because you and Adam want me in the dark doesn't mean anyone else does. There's a war, Emersyn's in the middle of this, and you and Adam are keeping secrets...including secrets about her."

His mouth flattened into a thin line.

"Go home, Ezra," I repeated. I would have to follow soon enough.

"Lainey," he said, catching my arm. I expected it, but I didn't pull away. He needed to see I was all right. His eyes narrowed more as he studied me. "Please... just come with me."

"Not yet," I said, then sighed. "There's more I need to do before I go...not more than a week."

He didn't like it. It was written all over his face. "One week?"

I didn't want to negotiate this, yet I also didn't dare leave it nebulous. One, he would never leave, and two...I already didn't want to go except that I had to. Pretty Boy was...

Covering his hand on my arm, I squeezed it. "One week."

He studied me for a long moment, then nodded once. I'll be back for you in a week."

"Come hell or high water?"

"If I have to burn the place down. Try to talk Emersyn into coming with us. You'll be happier if she's safer."

He wasn't wrong about that, although I was pretty sure she was safe right here.

"One week." When I pulled away, he let me go.

"I'll be waiting," he called, and I wasn't sure if it was a threat or a promise.

Probably both.

Pretty Boy straightened when I came out of the office and his thunderous expression wasn't encouraging. How the hell was I going to tell him goodbye?

FOURTEEN

MILO

"You know what happened." It wasn't a question. I followed Mayhem as she headed for the shower. She'd spent a big chunk of her day with Ivy, locked away in the dance studio. When they came out, they'd both been red-eyed, except neither had been in a sharing mood.

The guys were closing ranks around Ivy. As irritating as that behavior could seem, I respected their protectiveness of her. More, I valued it. For years, they'd helped me look after her from afar. Could I really fault them for wanting to protect her when she was right there?

I could, but I shouldn't.

No, I wouldn't.

Trying to get it all properly categorized in my brain was taking me more than a minute. All I wanted for Ivy was for her to be safe.

My life never had been. I needed hers to be.

Mayhem turned on the water before she began to strip off her clothes. I nudged the door shut, turning on the extractor and the heat lamp. It could be downright chilly in here, but I didn't want her getting too cold.

It wasn't long before she was nude. There were finger-prints on her hips from where I'd gripped her. I hadn't meant to squeeze so hard. As she turned, the flash of hickeys on her breasts made me smile.

Those...yeah, I'd meant every single one of those, as well as the pair I'd left inside her thighs. Exploring what made Mayhem scream could rapidly become my new calling in life.

"Don't look so smug," Mayhem told me in a droll tone. I grinned as she raised her brows, daring me to deny it.

"You enjoyed all of that," I said, both verifying for myself as well as teasing her.

"I absolutely did." Then she slid into the shower, leaving me to watch her behind the see-through curtain. As tempting as it was to climb in there, I leaned back against the counter to watch. Showering with someone was an intimacy you should be invited to share, not just assume.

We'd already taken several giant leaps without consul-tation. The fact she'd kept her virginity to herself was her right, but I loathed being the one who hurt her thought-lessly. I had tried to make it up to her in the meanwhile.

"Why are you scowling?" Mayhem asked, her tone almost plaintive, and it made my lips twitch. "A girl could get a complex with you scowling at her like that."

"A girl might," I said, letting the smile she provoked out. "However, you're not a girl. And your self-image isn't wrapped up in how I see you."

One of the many facets of Mayhem that I'd begun to truly appreciate over the last few days. She glanced at me over her shoulder as she reached for the shampoo. Slender, gentle curves, gorgeous hips, sweet breasts, and perfect lips...Mayhem was drop-dead gorgeous.

"I'm glad it doesn't bother you."

I chuckled, folding my arms and shaking my head. "I like it," I said.

"You didn't," she countered.

Sighing, I ran a hand over my jaw then shook my head. "I like a woman who knows her own value and doesn't need anyone to validate it. I appreciate it, not entirely used to it, although I am glad you have that strength."

Pivoting, she faced me. "What aren't you saying?"

The shoulder shrug wouldn't do for an answer. This was probably not the road to go down with her. Maybe especially with her.

"My mother wasn't that strong. When my father left, it destroyed her." It was hard to look back at her through the lens of adulthood. Mom had failed all of us. Me. Ivy. Herself. "My dad was a piece of shit. He used to deal drugs."

Surprise flared in her eyes.

"He had his own little enterprise." That was how I'd met Mickey. Mickey ran for him. Later, Mickey ran for some others. "Mom liked the product too much...when she got pregnant with Ivy, she got clean for a while. But...Dad never wanted another baby."

The ferocious look in his eye when he told Mom to get rid of "it." Ivy wasn't an it. She'd never been disposable. I didn't give a damn *what* he thought.

"The day he left, he said it was because she was useless and he had no interest in her or Ivy..." The son of a bitch wanted me to go with him. Shaking my head again, I tried to dislodge those old memories. I didn't tend to focus on him anymore.

After Mom died, I'd done my best to not think about

him again. I hadn't even named him. Ms. Steph and Mickey clearly knew who he was, but they'd kept it to themselves too. Even after Ivy had been adopted, I wanted nothing to do with the cold-hearted son of a bitch.

I found my new family, and they were the ones I was going to stick with.

"Fathers are overrated," Mayhem said in a considering tone that pulled all of my attention. "Not that I would know. I never met mine and his name isn't on the birth certificate. Whoever he was, my mother kept him a total secret. My grandfather, though..." Her expression transformed into a soft smile. "He's amazing."

"Well, your father is a dumbass if he didn't want to be in your life."

"Perhaps," she told me before tipping her head back into the water. "It might be that he wasn't given a choice. My mother does what she wants, doesn't care if she has to ask for forgiveness, but she will never ask for permission."

That explained some of Mayhem's ferociousness. But there was a heart in Mayhem, a deep and binding sense of loyalty that tied her to Ivy. A loyalty I respected because it was that loyalty that had bound the Vandals in the first place.

"I don't suppose I can convince you to tell me what Ivy has told you so far." I was pretty sure of the answer.

Mayhem didn't disappoint when she said, "No." No explanations, no apologies, and no attempt to even persuade me. She squeezed conditioner into her hand, then focused her attention on me. "Nevertheless, I do have some advice, if you want it."

"Do I want it?" I repeated the phrase, turning it over in my head. I'd have to be dead to not enjoy the view of her washing her hair, then running conditioner through it before she reached for a loofa and began to soap it up. Dead and buried. As it was, I also found the routine soothing. "I'd say I probably don't want it, but I need it. Ivy and I... we're still trying to work this out. I see my baby sister and she sees a stranger."

"She doesn't see a stranger," Mayhem told me as she washed her arms. "She sees a man who loves her without reservation and demand. She isn't totally sure what to do with that."

I frowned.

"She's never had a sibling. I have. There's a sense of acceptance and forgiveness that you have for everything she will ever do, because she is your sister."

Well, she wasn't wrong. I also bookmarked the bit about her sibling. Was there an older brother out there that would be coming to look for her?

"But Em? All she sees is the ways she might disappoint you. The fact you sent her away when she first met you... that hurt, Pretty Boy. I know you didn't intend for it too. Yet, it did hurt her."

I grimaced. No doubt existed within me that Mayhem knew more about all of this, that Ivy confided in her. While I wanted to demand that she tell me everything, I didn't.

I couldn't.

Especially after that last sentence. "I know," I admitted slowly. "I just...I want her safe."

"Well, maybe consider consulting her in her own safety. She's not your personal property to decide where she goes or who she sees."

My expression must have amused her because she laughed.

"Yes, I know it's hard when you think you know every-thing. But take it from someone kept perpetually in the dark. Eventually, the curtains are yanked open, and the light is blinding. You can't avoid all the pain in life, you can only arm yourself for it."

"She shouldn't—"

"Life isn't fair." Three words, so much meaning. "Life has *never* been fair. You don't get what you deserve. You get what you negotiate and fight for. Don't make her fight you to get what she needs. She will always have my first loyalty. Do I know more than I'm telling you? Yes. Will I tell you? Not without a damn good reason."

Fuck.

"Learn to listen to her. Not just hear her, but actually *listen* to what she tells you and how she tells you. If you love your sister as much as I see in your eyes...do not ever let the Sharpes near her again. *Any* of them."

I frowned.

"Don't trust them, Pretty Boy. Not her mother, her father, or her uncle. None."

I straightened at that warning; the slow, simmering anger in the pit of my stomach went volcanic. The whole family? *Why?*

"I can't give you any other answers," Mayhem told me, her gaze fixed on mine. "Except, I'm going to take care of setting up some accounts as soon as I get back. My trust fund is extensive, but much of it is locked up. Grandfather will help, and I can put aside an account for you and Em..."

"I don't want your money."

She shrugged one shoulder, before stepping beneath the spray to rinse off, including her hair. "I don't care. It's not about you or what you can and can't do for yourself or for her..."

I narrowed my eyes as she shut off the water. Reaching for a towel, I held it open for her and stepped to meet her as she climbed out of the shower. The warm steam and sweet scent of her sent lust to cleave through my earlier anger and annoyance.

"Then what is it about?" I asked, meeting her gaze. "Ivy?"

"Yes," she admitted. "That's part of it. I want to know she's safe and has what she needs. Accounts and access to funds are vital to that."

Wrapping the towel around her, I tugged her to me. I didn't give a damn about the water soaking my shirt or how flushed her face was as she peered up at me. I cared about feeling her. I cared about sinking into her and making her scream over and over.

"Okay."

"And...I'm leaving soon. So, it's better to take care of it now before—"

I didn't hear the rest of that statement. My brain snapped off when she said *leaving*.

What? "No," I told her. "You don't get to do that."

"Pretty Boy..."

I fisted the towel and kept her near me before dipping my head. "I said no, Mayhem. You stay here where I can keep you safe." Then I slammed my mouth down on hers. If she left...

No, I wouldn't allow it.

Her groan shattered my control as she looped her arms around my neck and I picked her up. I wasn't going to argue with her. Just fuck her until she couldn't walk.

Then fuck her some more if I had to.

Mayhem *couldn't* leave.

CHAPTER
FIFTEEN

LAINEY

The wall was almost too cold against my nipples, but a welcome relief to my heat-flushed body as Pretty Boy rocked into me. He had my hands trapped on the wall with one of his wrapped around my wrists. The heavy weight of his cock slamming into me was everything I could, and did, want.

With his free hand, he teased my clit. The sweat dripping down my face and over my chest shouldn't tantalize me so much. The feeling magnified when he pressed openmouth kisses along my throat. Arguing had never been so pleasurable...

Or heart-wrenching.

I strained to meet his thrusts. The rub of his thighs to mine, the bump of his hips to my ass, all seemed to accelerate my climb to the precipice. The gratification was right there—the simple, almost perfect rapture.

His breath was hot against my pulse point, every grunt that came from him as he pursued our release just added to my delight. Then I was orgasming, spasming around his cock as he kept going. The relentless drive caught me on my tumble down and sent me back up again.

Ever since he forgot the condom, he'd never gone back. The cum he'd already released into me earlier slicked his way and leaked onto my thighs, but it didn't discourage him. The flick of his fingers to my clit sent another pulse of wild pleasure rebounding through me. One orgasm crashed into the next, and when he finally let himself go, the hot jets of his cum seemed a decadence.

When he carried me down onto the bed, he kept his cock in me, his hand covering my pussy, and teased me where we were joined.

I'd died.

Or at least, I was pretty sure I'd died. The roughness of his fingers was just another tease to my already overstimulated senses. I drifted, half-floating, and then he was easing out of me. The loss was almost profound. The pressure of his fingers against my pussy roused me. He was pressing his cum back inside and when he lifted his slicked fingers to my lips, I cleaned them off.

Another groan escaped him, and then he chased the taste of himself from my lips with a kiss. "I have to go," he whispered. "Sleep."

It wasn't hard to agree to that. Exhaustion weighed me down. Every single time I'd brought up the fact I had to go, we'd ended up like this. My pussy was so sore, I wanted to complain, and at the same time, I craved his touch so fucking much.

He pressed another kiss to my shoulder and then slid off the bed. I lay there, half-drifting as he showered, changed, and then came back to brood over me. My eyes were mostly closed. It kept my secret while also preventing me from seeing his full expression.

The feather-light touch of his fingers down my cheek sent a shiver through me and then, all too soon, he was gone. Regret swarmed me in his absence as I pushed myself upright. Yeah, I was sore. The sensual aches a clear roadmap to every part of my body he'd explored.

I needed to go, and I didn't want to leave him or Em. Yes, this had started being about Em, but I'd be lying if I didn't say the affection and attachment I'd begun to develop for Pretty Boy wasn't also a problem.

No matter how much I wanted to stay, I couldn't. Andrea would be home any day, and I needed to be there for my baby sister. Reluctant and aching, I made my way to where my phone was hidden. I'd kept the burner phone powered off and tucked away for just such an occasion.

Pretty Boy wanted to take me back, or so he indicated. But that was just asking for more trouble. I could walk out the doors and leave on my own two feet, but Ezra's temper would only complicate things if I disappeared on everyone. So... I entered his number from memory.

He answered on the first ring. "Lainey?" The question in his voice tugged at me. Then again, he still answered even if he hadn't recognized the number.

"Yeah," I said. "You ready to come get me?"

"Thank fuck," he said with an exhale. "I'll be there in less than an hour."

He didn't wait for me to change my mind, just hung up. I showered, then pulled out my mostly packed bag from under the bed. I'd been putting it back together all week.

I did a quick, sketchy shower. Just enough to wash the smell of sex off and to get into clean clothes. I was going to be feeling Pretty Boy for days. The real problem with no condoms was that I'd be leaking for hours.

The thought made me clench up. Once I was ready, I went in search of Em. It didn't take me long to find her. This had been the plan all week, and she was the only one I'd told. I tried with Pretty Boy. I really did... Regret raked through me again.

"I really don't want you to go, no matter how much I know you have to," Emersyn said before wrapping her arms around me. I hugged her so damn tight. My best friend. The first sister I ever had.

"Same," I answered, blinking back the tears. This time with her had been everything. As damaged and hurting as she was, she was also fighting her way back.

"Thank you for helping them find me."

"Anytime," I said, sniffling despite myself. "However, I think never having to hunt for you again is a good plan."

"Deal."

I made a point of wiping away the tears before checking my watch. If Ezra was on time, he would be here in a minute. "Time to go."

"You're taking a car?" Emersyn asked as we stood, and I grabbed my bag.

"Something like that." Inviting Ezra could be a problem, but it was also the fastest way to cut this cord.

We walked out to the front. Vaughn glanced up from where he was working on a laptop in the living room, swept his gaze from Em to me, and then back again. "I thought you weren't leaving until tomorrow."

The question was definitely directed at me. I'd mentioned leaving in front of the others, when Pretty Boy couldn't fuck me into submission.

But there was nothing I could do about this. With Pretty

Boy gone, I needed to go as soon as possible. My phone buzzed with a message from Ezra.

Here. Let's go.

"My ride is here. You're walking us out, right?" I focused on Vaughn. Like every other Vandal orbiting Emersyn, his attention riveted on her.

"I'm just walking her to the car." She assured him. "No bolting for me."

The corner of his mouth kicked up, and he shut the laptop. "Yes, I'll be walking you both out there. Does Milo know you're leaving?"

I didn't answer him. Em let them make decisions and protect her. She balanced their primal responses with her own need to be cared for. That was fine. I was thrilled for her, didn't mean they got to exert any of that control over me.

The warehouse had people working, and a truck being offloaded. I ignored all of it and strode across to the door on the far side.

"You didn't tell him," Emersyn said as she fell into step with me.

I shook my head. "He wanted to take me back. That would not have gone over well."

The door we were en route to opened to let in Freddie. The mouthy guy amused me.

"Boo-Boo," he said, a grin twisting his lips when he spotted her. "Ball-Cracker."

Then he dropped his gaze to the bag.

"Oh, that explains the dickhead."

Dickhead...

The door behind Freddie jerked open and he didn't jump, almost like he'd been expecting it. Ezra filled the doorframe. He had never been patient.

"Ezra," I said as I closed on him. He dragged his gaze over me like he expected me to be injured or something, but I ignored it as he hooked the bag right from my fingers.

"You're both coming, right?"

"No," Vaughn warned from right behind Em. The red-haired tattoo artist was a big guy. Even Ezra seemed to take that into account. "Not even sure *she* should be going with you."

Instead, he focused on me. "Come on, the car's outside, and we're going before any more of those assholes show up." He spared one last look at Em. "Are you sure you don't want to go?"

"She's sure," Freddie said abruptly in a violently unfriendly tone. "Just like I told you outside."

The tension crackled in the air, and I paused, but Ezra kept himself between them and me.

"I'm fine. I promise." Emersyn assured him. "I'm not leaving."

"Oh my god," I said with a snap, barely resisting the urge to smack him. The point of him picking me up was so we could get in the car and speed away. Not start another violent confrontation. "Leave her alone, Ezra. I told you when I called that you were just picking *me* up. If you're going to be an asshole about it, I'll get a rideshare or something."

"The hell you will," he snarled as he jerked his head back to look at me. "You're going back with me and staying with me. No more crazy schemes or going off on your own."

I just glared at him, but Em marched right up and poked him in the chest.

"Be nice to her, or I'll be the one kicking your ass. You don't have to be a dick *all* the time. We know you were worried."

"Do you?" he countered, not backing off in the slightest. "Do you even know who these people are around you or the war that's going on?"

"War?" I rolled my eyes. She had enough on her plate, and I did not want him terrifying her. "Stop being so dramatic. You're here because you already had one freak-out, and I need a ride. Don't make me regret calling you…"

"Come with us," Ezra said, dropping his voice. "You two are happier in the same place anyway—it makes it easier to keep you both safe."

The genuine concern in his tone dried up my sarcasm and irritation. Ezra really did care about Em. Maybe not like me, but he wanted to help her *for* me and that counted—

"Get your fucking hands off my sister." There was no mistaking the warning in Pretty Boy's voice. "Who the hell invited you here, anyway?"

Ezra suddenly pulled Em to us and shoved her back with me.

Pretty Boy wasn't alone; there were more Vandals.

"Ezra, stop," I said, gripping his jacket and tugging. "I mean it. I want to go now. We need to leave."

I didn't dare look at Pretty Boy. "You called him?"

"Yes," I said. "You have things to do, and I have a life to return to. So, I suggest both of you boys put your dicks away. I'll be in the car." I dropped my hand to Ezra's pocket and slid his keys out. I could not stand here in the middle of this. I didn't want to see the regret or the hurt on Pretty Boy's face.

When I looked at Em, she grabbed my fallen bag. "Freddie, can you walk us out? I'll be right back."

I didn't turn around to look at the standoff. I wasn't a coward, but I'd been fighting myself all week. I couldn't fight all of us.

"Go on, Sparrow, walk your friend out. We'll take care of this."

Freddie glided out ahead of us, holding the door. The cold air washed over me as I headed straight for the black Mercedes. Popping the trunk, I took my bag from Em and put it in there before starting the engine with the remote. When I reached for her, she collided with me.

The hug was everything I needed.

"Be careful," she whispered.

"You, too."

Then the door slammed open, and Ezra stalked toward us. I let Em go, and it was a good thing, because he scooped me right up and over his shoulder. Fucking boys.

When he put me down next to the passenger side, I slammed my elbow into his stomach. He grunted. But the heat in his eyes left very little room for argument.

After he opened the door, I slid inside on my own. He looked down at me, relief softening his expression before he glanced back to where Em stood.

"Still time to come..."

"I meant it. This is my home now."

"If that changes, you just have to call."

"Just look after Lainey, please," she told him.

"I *always* do." He closed my door then circled around to the driver's seat. I'd just snapped my seatbelt on when Freddie leaned sideways to wave at me.

"See ya, Ball-Cracker!"

I really didn't have a chance to say anything because Ezra was already accelerating before his door fully closed. The engine purred as he raced out of the alley and onto the street. When I glanced at him, he cut his head in a hard shake.

"Not one word, Lainey," he said. "Not one word."

I snorted. "Or what?"

The dark look he shot sent me the first real shiver of apprehension. I usually only saw that side of him when he was drunk.

"You're going to find out."

EPILOGUE

EZRA

The phone rang as we reached the airport. I took one look at the King's contact information and declined the call. I didn't care what he wanted or why he wanted it. As it was, the plane waited for me on a private runway. The crew were all hand-picked by me. They were all people I could trust.

I didn't bother to find a lot for the car. Instead, I drove right to the doors. Lainey frowned, but I didn't comment as I threw the car into park and then stalked out to circle it and open her door. She glared up at me.

"Get out of the car," I told her, keeping my tone as even and as civil as I could. She'd gone off on some wild adventure with that group of criminals Liam was so busy protecting he'd left Adam to take the fall for him. I wasn't going to lose Lainey the same way. I didn't care if it pissed her off.

Better angry than dead.

"I asked for a ride home, not—"

The protest was enough for me. I reached in, unsnapped her seatbelt and then hauled her out of the car. She was up and over my shoulder before she realized what I was doing. We made it three steps before she started struggling.

I landed three, swift and hard slaps to her ass that stilled her protests. "Behave, Lainey, or I will bare this ass right here and spank it until it's red." She froze.

"You wouldn't—"

"Dare me," I told her. "Please."

Because right now, I had no limits.

Thirty seconds of absolute silence.

"Pity," I spit out the last two syllables. "I'm sure we'll be able to do this again." She was too stubborn for anything else. I stalked across the tarmac to where my men waited. The pilot said nothing as I carried her on board.

As soon as I dumped her in a seat, I buckled her in and accepted the wine glass from the fight attendant who said nothing about Lainey's harried expression or tumble of hair. It was hard to miss the hickeys on her neck or the hint of swollen lips.

She'd taken one of those assholes for a lover.

If I had to bet money, I knew which one.

Fine.

I'd kill him later.

Tossing back the wine and wishing it was vodka, I glanced at the captain. "Get us in the air."

"Of course, Mr. Graham." The crew did their jobs swiftly and the whole time, I stood right over Lainey. No one was talking to her and no one was taking her away. I didn't sit until all exterior doors were closed. Then I took the seat next to hers.

When the captain announced the flight time, Lainey snapped her gaze to me. "What are you doing?"

"What I have to," I told her.

"I have to go home, Ezra," she said and I leaned back in the seat. "I have to go back to New York..."

"You should have thought of that before."

"I had to go," she snapped at me. "Em needed me, I had to be there."

"You did what you had to do," I said as the plane raced up the runway. "Now, so am I."

Their story will continue in Battle Lines,
Book Two of Bay Ridge Royals

AFTERWORD

Don't worry, we're far from done with Lainey and Milo. Some of their story can be seen in 82nd Street Vandals, but a full series is coming this fall with Battle Lines kicking off book 2 of 6 in the Bay Ridge Royals.

xoxo

Heather

P.S. Yes, it will be why choose/reverse harem.

Reader group:
facebook.com/groups/heatherspack
Spoiler group:
facebook.com/groups/teammadatheather

BATTLE LINES
BAY RIDGE ROYALS BOOK 1

Violence chose me a long time ago...

Survival isn't everything. I've fought to protect my family. I've bled for them, killed for them, and gone to jail for them. There is no fight I will not take on for them...

I've been waging this war since I was seven years old. The only thing that's changed is the battlefield itself.

For Mayhem, I'll trade in the grime of the streets for the illusions of her shimmering world. Only all that glitter is hiding a well of sin and corruption that leaves blood in its wake. This isn't my world, but I won't be defeated by it.

I may have lost battles before, but I won't lose this one. If that means I have to drown in darkness, then it's a price I'm willing to pay.

Order

About Heather Long

I *love* books. Not just a little bit, but a lot. Books were my best friends when I was growing up. Books didn't care if I was new to a town or to a class. They were always there, my trustiest of companions. Until they turned on me and said I had to write them.

I can tell you that my own personal happily ever after included writing books. I've always said that an HEA is a work in progress. It's true in my marriage, my friendships, and in my career. I am constantly nurturing my muse as we dive into new tales, new tropes, new characters and more.

After seventeen years in Texas, we relocated to the Pacific Northwest in search of seasons, new experiences, and new geography. I can't wait to discover what life (and my muse) have in store for me.

Maybe writing was always my destiny and romance my fate. After all, my grandmother wasn't a fan of picture books and used to read me her Harlequin Romance novels.

Follow Heather & Sign up for her newsletter:
www.heatherlong.net
TikTok

ALSO BY HEATHER LONG

82nd Street Vandals

Savage Vandal

Vicious Rebel

Ruthless Traitor

Dirty Devil

Shamelessly Loyal (Novella)

Brutal Fighter

Dangerous Renegade

Merciless Spy

Reckless Thief

Fierce Dancer

Always a Marine Series

Once Her Man, Always Her Man

Retreat Hell! She Just Got Here

Tell It to the Marine

Proud to Serve Her

Her Marine

No Regrets, No Surrender

The Marine Cowboy

The Two and the Proud

A Marine and a Gentleman

Combat Barbie

Whiskey Tango Foxtrot

What Part of Marine Don't You Understand?

A Marine Affair

Marine Ever After

Marine in the Wind

Marine with Benefits

A Marine of Plenty

A Candle for a Marine

Marine under the Mistletoe

Have Yourself a Marine Christmas

Lest Old Marines Be Forgot

Her Marine Bodyguard

Smoke & Marines

Bay Ridge Royals

Shamelessly Loyal (Novella)

Battle Lines

Blue Ivy Prep

Problem Child

Mad Boys

Party Crashers

Money Shot

Bravo Team Wolf

When Danger Bites

Bitten Under Fire

Cardinal Sins

Kill Song

First Chorus

High Note

Last Word

Chance Monroe

Earth Witches Aren't Easy

Plan Witch from Out of Town

Bad Witch Rising

Her Elite Assets

Featuring:

Pure Copper

Target: Tungsten

Asset: Arsenic

Fevered Hearts

Marshal of Hel Dorado

Brave are the Lonely

Micah & Mrs. Miller

A Fistful of Dreams

Raising Kane

Wanted: Fevered or Alive

Wild and Fevered

The Quick & The Fevered

A Man Called Wyatt

Heart of the Nebula

Queenmaker

Deal Breaker

Throne Taker

Lone Star Leathernecks

Semper Fi Cowboy

As You Were, Cowboy

Shackled Souls

Succubus Chained

Succubus Unchained

Succubus Blessed

Shackled Souls (Omnibus)

Space Cowboy

Space Cowboy Survival Guide

Untouchable

Rules and Roses

Changes and Chocolates

Keys and Kisses

Whispers and Wishes

Wolves of Willow Bend

His Moonstruck Wolf

Thunder Wolf

Ghost Wolf

Outlaw Wolves

Wolf Unleashed